To John
– Enjoy

D1534884

BAD REPUTATION

A NOVEL

MATT HADER

Matt Ha [signature]

ThinkBox Publishing • Vancouver, Canada

BAD REPUTATION

Published By

THINKBOX PUBLISHING
a division of ThinkBox Entertainment Ltd.
1027 Davie Street, Suite 235
Vancouver, BC.
Canada, V6E 4L2

Library and Archives Canada Cataloguing in Publication

Hader, Matt, 1960-
Bad reputation / Matt Hader.

Issued also in electronic format.
ISBN 978-0-9876986-2-9

I. Title.

PS3608.A26B34 2011 813'.6 C2011-906514-2

For Lori Bowling...

Acknowledgments

First, I want to thank my parents, Joan and Art Hader for their love and guidance throughout the years. You two are the most entertaining people I know. Also, I want to acknowledge my siblings (say this as quickly as you can so that you can become part of an inside family joke) Art, John, Bill, Dan, Missy, Rick, and Andy for unknowingly providing me with all sorts of material (I kid). I am grateful for Rob Chapin and his wonderful mother, Barb, who helped me to find my own creative voice, and to Bernie Brady for his lifelong friendship and for all the times we exploded illegal fireworks in the alley behind his house. Thanks to my friend, Diane dos Santos, for her editorial mojo and Lew Wietzman for his guidance. I am indebted to Pat DiNizio for his camaraderie and professional encouragement and to Jason Pila whose brotherly friendship and professional support always kept me on track. But I especially want to thank my sons, Matt and Shane – and my lovely wife, Lori. I love you all very much and couldn't do this stuff without you!

"That guy is a lowlife scummy little fat rat weasel bastard… But I don't mean that in a bad way."

– Dom Irrera

CHAPTER

- 1 -

It wasn't that John Caul didn't want to be where he was at the moment - inside the dingy, medical suite in Lake Zurich, Illinois, pointing a cheap 9mm pistol at the dentist's head - he was simply conflicted.

He was happy to know that he was closer to raising enough money to anonymously save his town's famous Fourth of July Festival from being cancelled. It was the longest-running such festival in the Chicago area. Just ask any one of the proud residents in John's hometown of Balmoral, and they'd gladly tell you all about it.

How it all started back in the 1880's as a one-day event and slowly, over the years, morphed into the week-long extravaganza it had grown to be. They'd talk about the multiple parades, beer tents, the live bands, and of course, the fireworks display that would last for over 30 minutes.

Most fireworks displays in the Chicago suburbs would carry on for about 15 minutes. But if you wanted to see multi-colored palm tree, waterfall, and red, white and blue mortar fireworks for a solid half hour straight, Balmoral was the only place to be at 10 p.m. on any given Fourth of July.

What was troubling John, as the dentist dumped several bundles of $20 bills from a small strongbox out onto the front counter, was that he was truly frightening the dental office receptionist.

The poor woman couldn't keep from nervously gulping as she took in the sight of John, his gun and the plastic, see-through, "baby face" mask he was wearing. The baby face on the outside frozen in a creepy smile, but John sporting a middle of the road expression underneath. That juxtaposition seemed to unnerve Amy, the receptionist.

A minute or so earlier, as the whole scenario began, John didn't scream, yell or make idle threats. He basically walked in, pointed the gun at the dentist and said, "The money and all the Vikes you have."

Cool. Calm. No drama.

That's how John had been doing all the robberies leading up to this point - professional and violence-free.

The dentist's office didn't fit into his ultimate, and quickly hatched, master plan of robbing only cash-laden breakfast restaurants, but he had to be open to fresh opportunities when they presented themselves. And this time, it was going much more smoothly than the first robbery he pulled off a month earlier. That happened the day after he initially heard that his town was cancelling the Fourth of July celebration.

John's first robbery went down at a high-end hair salon in Deer Park. The salon, with some French-spelled name, was located in the middle of a wide-arching Lifestyle Center off of Route 12.

"Lifestyle center, mall, whatever," thought John as he noticed the number of Land Rovers and Mercedes Benzes parked in front. He thought, "So what if it isn't a cash-rich breakfast joint?" He knew that it was right.

He collected the money and corralled all of the hair salon

employees, and a half-dozen pampered housewives, into a massage therapy room occupied by a naked and panicky, chubby woman awaiting a hot mud treatment.

After leaving his victims, some sporting foil wrapped hair and cotton between their freshly manicured toes, packed into the tiny room, John was confronted by the biggest woman he had ever seen.

Her spa nameplate read "Gretchen – Shampoo Tech," but her dead-eyed expression and wide shoulders screamed "outside linebacker." For her size, she could really move. She had what the head coach of her Muscatine, Iowa high school football team called "natural football speed." She had quick feet, was agile and aggressive, and she was really, really big.

Gretchen was named as an all-conference linebacker her junior year of high school, but blew out her right knee while playing volleyball during the off season. She never saw any more play on the gridiron. Six months ago, her husband of three years had left her for another woman.

And now, all these months later, Gretchen was still looking for a valid excuse to pile-drive someone into the ground. She desperately needed to release some pent-up tension, and she reckoned that this moron in the mask would be the perfect candidate.

John was quicker than Gretchen, though. Juking right, a head fake, heading left, grabbing up the tip box off the front counter and he was gone, leaving Gretchen crumbling painfully to her bad knee and crawling toward the phone.

For John's hometown, like many of the municipalities surrounding Chicago, these were tough economic times, complete with lowered homeowner tax revenues. A killer scenario for any planned, community activities, especially an expensive one like a huge Fourth of July celebration.

Instead of simply cutting back on the celebration from a week-long event to a day or two, which they had the money to do, the Balmoral Village council members decided to throw out the baby with the bathwater and cancel the entire soirée. If they couldn't do it right, they were not going to do it at all.

But in Lake Zurich, things were looking up.

The dentist said, "Just take it and go."

John swiped the money off the counter and into a crumpled, plastic grocery bag in one motion and said, "I bet the cops would love to know why a dentist has so much cash on hand."

The dentist froze in place, his mouth working but no words coming out.

John had heard through what he called the "Vike vine," a loose grouping of Vicodin addicts in the Northwest suburbs who swapped coded bits of information via Twitter on where to score, pricing and other illegal Vicodin consumer news, that the dentist was the top provider in the area.

In a bit of kismet, the dentist was located in Lake Zurich, a mere three miles from John's home. It was all about the Vicodin, cash and convenience. It was a winning combination for John.

"The Vikes?"

The dentist, now sporting a completely defeatist attitude, nodded for John to follow him into the back room. John motioned for the terrified Amy to come along, which she reluctantly did. Amy was a very pretty woman in her thirties, but so frightened now, her eyes red from crying and her face contorting at ugly angles.

The dentist led John to a back room and a large built-in cabinet. "I'll figure out who you are, you know," he said as he unlocked the cabinet.

John smiled under the mask and said, "That's the plan."

As John admired the confused look he had just helped to place on the dentist's face, Amy scrambled from the room.

But John didn't give chase.

He didn't even acknowledge her departure. He simply loaded up as many bottles of Vicodin as he could hold in his pockets, a fresh grocery bag and his hands, and left.

CHAPTER
-2-

In that space, where the blue sky meshed with the greenery of the fully-blossomed trees, *John* was a bit hazy from the 500 mg of Vicodin doing its magic on his nervous system - and vision.

It was the aroma that was most intoxicating, though.

While probably important, it wasn't really the joy of volunteering that led John to mowing this particular field; it was mostly the smell of freshly cut grass in springtime. It was just the thing to completely wipe away the winter blues.

The small riding mower John operated made perfect crisscrossing cuts on the well-maintained, little league ball field. The mower's raging motor roar was drowned out by his iPod earbuds cranking The Smithereens' "Blues Before and After."

Balmoral, like most towns of its stature, was a prideful community, pleased with its neighborhoods, the vibrant little downtown, and charming historical district. But, in 1990, the town was most self-satisfied with their two-time defending state championship high school basketball team and the brand-new gym that was recently dedicated and about to be put into use.

The gym was huge - double the seating capacity of the old

one. There was a large scoreboard, complete with a Jumbo Tron-like screen on one wall and padded VIP seats in the middle section of the home stands.

John was a senior there at the time, and two days before the start the 1990 basketball season, he accidentally burned the brand-new gym to the ground. The shellacked hardwood floor of the basketball court was a polished beauty, but it acted like a hardened sheen of napalm the moment the arcing, stage lighting equipment John was working near lit it up.

John, while almost being killed by the flames and acrid smoke, barely escaped the conflagration and managed to pull several fire alarms as he sprinted for the exit. All of the 1,200 occupants of the high school, students and staff alike, escaped without harm. But the basketball team seemed cursed after that and never saw a winning season again.

The building was insured, and rebuilt, but the accident gnawed at John. Some of the locals didn't let him forget about it, either, not even 20 years later.

"Hey, Sparky, you missed a spot!"

John, the earbuds firmly in place, didn't quite make out what the smartass teenager said, but by the smug expression on the teen's face, he completely understood. John faked a smile and waved. He was used to fake smiling when confronted by one of the wiseass locals. He went about his work as the teenager plodded away, trying to keep his baggy pants from slipping down over his SpongeBob SquarePants boxer shorts.

But a real smile returned to John's face as he thought about the soon-to-be-saved Fourth of July celebration. It was a bookend grin compared to the one from the day before, when he dropped the thick, white envelope containing most of the bundled $20s from the dentist's office in the Balmoral municipal building lobby. Inside the envelope with the money was a hand printed "Save the Celebration" note. He nestled the money into the little wicker basket on the counter alongside a smattering of village resident's paid water bills.

No one actually saw John drop the money off because most in town ignored him. It wasn't that he was an ugly or unhygienic man. Just the opposite was true. At a lean 6'1" with dark brown hair and boyish good looks, John was someone the women from other towns would tend to check out, just not the majority of ladies from John's neighborhood.

"Burned it down by accident, my ass," said Lou in his Greek-influenced, broken English. He watched from the front window of his diner as John made his way into the municipal building across the street. Lou didn't know it, but John had the thick cash-filled envelope in his back pocket.

Lou was the owner of Dink's Diner, a town staple since 1949. He had taken over ownership 25 years earlier after working as the cook for a time. The diner's name came from the tiny size of the establishment. It was no more than 10 feet wide by 30 feet long on the interior of the old building, and that included the kitchen space. But the food was excellent and that kept the customers coming back time after time.

The diner was also the place where the locals got the true, inside scoop on the news behind the local news. If a businessman from town had been caught up in an ugly IRS audit, or a Balmoral politician cheated on his or her spouse, Dink's Diner was the place where that news would break first. It was a quality food-serving version of CNN in Balmoral.

Lou peered through the diamond-shaped window in the door of his business, just as John stepped out from the municipal building and made his way past the dry cleaners.

Lou opened the front door of his establishment and spit into the street, "That fucker knew exactly what he was doing." And that right there was the prevailing attitude toward John all these twenty years later. The chuckles and belittling remarks from the other diner patrons confirmed it.

"Worthless piece of shit is all he is," said Emil, one of the daily regulars. Emil was a cantankerous, 80-year-old man who rarely suffered fools, especially John. He had a special hate for

John Caul because he had always blamed him for his own son's retreat from the world of success-seekers.

His son, Spencer, was two years younger than John and a standout guard on the basketball team his sophomore year at Balmoral High School. By the time he made the varsity squad his junior year, the basketball team had started their 20-year-long losing slide.

Spencer wound up not being the lawyer or doctor, or whatever, that Emil had planned for him to be, though. Right after he graduated from high school, Spencer got a gig as a mailman. But that allowed him to pursue his passion of playing the guitar. These days Spencer would clock out at his day job and trade his USPS blue uniform for ratty jeans and a Fender guitar, playing the local roadhouses for chump change.

Emil believed that John's burning down of the gym was the reason for his son's perceived decline. While the gym was being rebuilt, the basketball squad had to play all of their games "away," in their rivals' gymnasiums. Without the proper fan support, the team took the nose dive they still endured to this day.

"If only Spencer played in that brand-new, magnificent gym in the 90's, having all those people cheer him on, he would've become something," Emil would say to anyone who would listen.

"I've never seen that guy do any real work, unless you count him riding his little mower all around town," chimed in another regular.

Lou stepped away from the door, and said, "Don't know how he survives."

Emil added, "I heard he scrounges through dumpsters for food."

Larry, the dreadlock-wearing and overly-tattooed African-American cook, shook his head, and thought to himself, chuckling, "These assholes know for fuck-sure that John eats in this place at least once a week."

Larry liked John.

He was one of the few in Balmoral who would actually seek

out a conversation with the town's outcast.

You would also think that town officials would be on the lookout for "the money dropper," but they weren't. In fact, only a few council members even knew about someone leaving just one singular, anonymous gift, and they weren't talking too much about it.

There was, though, one village official, a man named Keith Michaels, who knew about all of the money being left surreptitiously in the municipal building lobby. The reason he knew about the money being left was because he had taken it all for himself without anyone else knowing.

The inept village council members, their ranks comprised of proctologists, dentists, and real estate agents looking for additional PR and patients for their practices, were unaware that someone was trying to save them from the poor financial moves they had made three years earlier. That's when the majority of the council decided to sink the entire village budget surplus into the stock market through a Lehman Brothers' representative that one of the council members knew.

It was a classic case of a "golfing buddy gone wrong."

After no one had made a move to stop him following this latest donation, John chalked it up to the town officials being too proud to admit that they couldn't save the celebration themselves. That made his giving all the more satisfying.

What John didn't realize was that Keith Michaels, a real estate agent by trade, was taking the money as soon as it was dropped. And to date, only one envelope and note had been found by the other council members. It was only a few thousand dollars and hardly enough to put a dent in paying for the Fourth of July Festival so the council members weren't allowing that news to travel outside their chambers. For now, no one else in town would be aware of the attempt to save the festival.

***

Keith Michaels, a man with all the physical and emotional

attributes of a pet marmot, had discovered the first envelope when he noticed how thick it was – much larger than the normal water bill payments that usually resided in the wicker basket on the counter in the municipal building lobby.

Balmoral was that type of town. It was a place where residents could safely place their paid village utility bills in a basket in the public area of the municipal building. Anyone could snatch them - but they didn't.

Keith also noticed that the envelope was white and not the light gray color of the water bill envelopes. It was after hours, and he had time to rifle through the thick envelope without being discovered.

In fact, Keith had made a nightly habit of fingering through all of the envelopes in the wicker basket to make sure some fool hadn't placed cash inside to pay their water bill. He used care in opening each envelope and resealing them with a glue stick so that he wouldn't be found out. That's how he had discovered the first of the robbery proceeds.

Keith needed cash. And fast.

The unscrupulous Oak Park investor he owed $50,000 was counting on him as well.

Keith wanted so badly to be successful and to get out from under the shadow of his father-in-law, who was a self-made multi-millionaire in the heating and air-conditioning trade. Keith had to cut some legal corners to make that happen, too.

It had all started when he located a parcel of land for sale near the Randall Road shopping district in the far northwest suburbs. Randall Road was the current popular shopping destination, not for its upscale shops, but for the sheer number of retail outlets located in the mile-long stretch of road near Algonquin.

Keith was going to make the deal to prove to his father-in-law that he had developed brilliant business acumen. He could decide later whether to raise the additional capital to build retail centers on the land or sell the parcel at a huge profit to another party who would then build on the land.

Keith Michaels used the "Baby Face Robber's" funds to purchase the property. Well, he didn't know it was the "Baby Face Robber's" money, but he took it anyway. He also used funds from his and his wife's own savings account, and the $50,000 he received from a 52-year-old Oak Park man named Franky "Five Bucks."

Franky "Five Bucks" was raised in the Little Italy neighborhood on Chicago's Near West Side. Franky, born Frederik Gregers, the son of an immigrant fish monger, stood out like a blonde-haired, blue-eyed sore thumb in the predominantly Italian American area. His choppy Danish accent, which was now mixed with a distinctive Chicago intonation, didn't help his cause at first, either.

His father, Jorgen, had an incredible eye for quality seafood, and a penchant for negotiating the best prices from wholesalers. Because he consistently stocked the best seafood at the lowest prices, Jorgen Gregers was widely welcomed into the Italian neighborhood.

Young Frederik soon learned that to fit into the dog-eat-dog West Side neighborhood, he needed an edge over some of the other, much stronger and fearless, area dwellers of his age group. He smartly decided to use his intelligence to get ahead in the world. As a young teenager, and like most of the other kids his age, he lacked the brawn needed to make a name for himself, though. Using a gun wasn't his style, either. But he would soon be able to hire the muscle to get his way.

Like his old man, Frederik had a knack for negotiating. His deals, though, usually revolved around the buying and/or selling of something, really anything, for $5. Whether it be the ten dozen donuts he snatched from the unattended back door of a bakery, or the blow job he procured from a local whore, $5 was the usual end point to the then 14-year-old Frederik's business dealings.

Everyone in Frederik's area of Chicago had a nickname. He was a huge Sinatra fan so soon enough Frederik Gregers became Franky "Five Bucks." Normally the others in the neighborhood would provide the cool, and sometimes not-so-cool, nicknames for the various inhabitants. Frederik caused a minor, but not long-lasting stir by supplying his own moniker.

A home inspector and poker playing buddy of Keith's introduced him to Franky "Five Bucks." At first Keith appreciated Franky "Five Bucks" seemingly jovial nature. He was quite the jokester. For a loan shark/bookie, he was okay. After Keith discussed his need for funding and the sweet deal he had gotten on the Randall Road property, Franky "Five Bucks" wanted in. He'd loan Keith Michael's $50,000 and get back $150,000 for his troubles.

The $100,000 Keith was paying for the two-acre parcel was a steal. Keith could not believe his luck in locating the deal.

The current owner of the property was an 87-year-old farmer named Len Cramer. Cramer had lived on the property for years, and grew corn there up until his knees went out and he couldn't continue working. That was last year.

When the Randall Road building craze began, he started selling off parcels of his 300-acre farm. The two acres that Keith purchased were the last bits of land that Len owned, and it was where his 100-year-old farm house was located, which was currently positioned next to the loading dock of a Bed Bath & Beyond.

The going rate of an acre was nearly one million in the Randall Road area. Keith felt like he was taking advantage of the old man, but needed to make this deal to show the world, and mostly his father-in-law, that he was not a complete putz.

There were two major problems with Keith's plan, though. One was that his wife wasn't aware of the missing money from their joint savings account – money that was given to her by her parents. And two, the land he purchased was incorrectly zoned as commercial. He was given that tidbit of information just two days after he closed on the property when a McHenry County zoning official caught up to him at his Balmoral real estate office. They were the real estate offices that were owned by his wife and her parents.

The McHenry County zoning official didn't enjoy telling Keith how the former zoning official, a man he had taken over for a week before, had been on the take. He was mislabeling several of the parcels in the Randall Road area as "commercial" and taking bribes from the current landowners, so they could rope in rubes like Keith.

That little old man, Len Cramer, had fucked Keith Michaels over and was now enjoying himself and his brand-new, 42-year-old girlfriend, in the condo he purchased on Marco Island, Florida.

So the acreage purchased was adjacent to, but could never become part of, the huge shopping district that lined both sides of the wide boulevard known as Randall Road. There was a third problem, as well. The economy tanked three weeks after the money was turned over, and the land became his.

Keith Michaels was the proud owner of two acres of barely usable land, and $100,000 in the hole, to boot. $50,000 of that debt was now owed to the formerly jovial Franky "Five Bucks." And Franky still wanted the additional $100,000 that was negotiated in the initial deal. A deal was a deal.

***

If you had asked John a year before if he'd ever do something like rob businesses in neighboring municipalities so he could save his own town's famous Fourth of July celebration, he would have laughed. But something happened when the economy turned and his town hit a financial rough patch.

People became even crueler and began openly taking their frustrations out on him at an accelerated pace. He was an easy target because everyone knew that the only reason he volunteered in the first place was due to his guilt over accidentally burning down the high school gym.

Even the cashiers at the Gemstone Grocery Store on Main Street would display their "out of service" placards when they saw him rolling his packed shopping cart their way. John became a whiz at the self-checkout lane, faster than the cashiers who ignored him.

The thoughts of past confrontations in town looped endlessly in John's mind. He could see and hear the townsfolk yelling at him from across the expanse of a grocery store or the street. The agitators never really got right up into his face, though. They were brutal but usually from a distance.

And the eggings got worse.

A few times a month, John would wake to thumping sounds at the front of his house late at night. He knew exactly what the thumps were, but never got out of bed. In the morning, he'd wake to the sight of splattered eggs on the windows, the front walls, and the sidewalk leading up to his tiny porch. No matter the weather, someone got it in their head to egg his house. Even on Christmas.

At first he tried scraping, cleaning, and sometimes repainting the tougher egg stains, but not any longer. His house wore the stains like proud battle scars. That made his property stand out all the more - where teardowns replaced by McMansions was the norm, and the tiny, post-war frame houses like John's were the anomaly.

The dried eggs made John's house appear as if it was a guano-covered rock in the middle of a tree lined suburban paradise.

His dwelling may have looked like hell, but the neighbors had stopped complaining years ago because John refused to bow to their demands. No village fine would change him from not painting or repairing his home. And now, even the neighbors would ignore John whenever they saw him outside his home. It was as if he didn't even exist – and that was fine with him.

In the early 1980's, before the teardown/rebuild craze began, John was the cock of the roost in his neighborhood. He was an excellent athlete, outgoing, and a leader among the other neighborhood kids, even at the tender age of 11.

He was a nice kid, but other youngsters in the neighborhood who ever attempted to embarrass or challenge him learned quickly that John could fight if backed into a corner. He would make quick work of any foolish neighborhood bullies who crossed the line with him.

John and his best friend, Rob, already a contrarian by nature, for all of his ten or so years on earth, were inseparable. Rob never shied away from mouthing off to any elder who tried to slide any sort of wisdom or advice his way. Rob contradicted first; asked questions, never. He already thought that he knew it all.

John and Rob got into some trouble from time to time. Like when they were caught clipping the hood ornament off a brand-new Mercedes Benz that was parked on their block. Or the time they crafted a persnickety neighbor's vine-covered trellis into an aluminum pretzel after the neighbor kept a football of theirs that had been inadvertently tossed into his yard.

John and Rob received the punishment they deserved each time they messed up - usually a crack across the back of the head for Rob from his old man, and for John, a long freeze-out by his disapproving mother, Mary.

John's mom never laid a hand on him or his older brother. It wasn't that she didn't discipline the boys. She simply had a different approach than some of the other parents in the neighborhood.

Here's how the punishment usually played out. First, the offender was banished to the plastic-covered living room sofa for most of the day without any television privileges. There they would have to watch as their mother went about her daily chores, all the while being totally ignored by her.

The perp suffered from torture by boredom. It was an effective deterrent for kid crime.

And it got worse.

At the dinner table, John's mother would sport what John and his brother would call "the look." It wasn't a scary expression, just that well-worn, dour and disapproving face only a mother can exact on a child. The look was usually accompanied by her withholding any further attention toward the offender for a length of time, usually a day or so.

John's dad, on the other hand, was a comic-wannabe.

Bernie Caul would try to diffuse any difficult situation with a sophomoric joke and a dopey grin. John had no respect for him or the idiotic and corresponding to the "kid crime," knock-knock jokes he improvised. It usually just made the situations worse.

"Knock-knock."

John would reluctantly play along, "Who's there?"

"Don Cha."

"Don Cha, who?"

"Don Cha you do the crime if you can't do the time, Sport."

John hated his dad.

He often fantasized about having Rob's parents for his own. At least they paid attention to the contrarian Rob by cracking him across the back of the head when he fucked up. But with Rob, that was it. The punishment was dispensed, and the situation was over. He could go about his carefree kid day.

At John's house, alternatively, there was silence from his mother on one side, and from the other, his dad, who everyone called "Shecky," spewing inane jokes. It all equated to the waterboarding of an 11-year-old kid in 1980's Balmoral.

The one and only thing that truly brought his family together each and every year, was the fabulous Balmoral Fourth of July Festival.

For the entire week that the event lasted his mother and father were sincerely interested in what John and his older brother were doing. It could have been because both his parents had been raised in the town and were trying to recapture a bit of their own carefree youth, but John wasn't sure.

He chose never to question the good feelings that washed over their tiny home on Coleridge Avenue when Fourth of July rolled around each summer. He was always glad for the festival's arrival.

Groundbreaking on the first McMansion in his neighborhood took place the week after John's mother's funeral. It was the summer that he turned 13. Rob and his family moved out of the area soon after, wanting to take advantage of the money being paid for their highly sought after building lots.

Right after his mother's passing, John had gone "Goth." He fell into the Goth line by wearing black clothing, died jet-black hair, black fingernail polish - the whole "dark arts" getup.

Life after his mother's death and Rob's departure became as dim as his wardrobe. Little by little, the carefree existence of youth was draining from him.

That joyless way of life accelerated after he learned that his friend, Rob, had been killed. He had stolen a canoe from a home along the Des Plaines River, fell out of the boat, and drowned after getting caught in the powerful undertow of a low-water dam.

At his high school, John was a total outcast. He would stand out like a shadow man among the bright clothing and toothy smiles of the well-to-do Balmoral youth.

Although they tried at first, any possible bully that John encountered was swiftly repelled by his bursts of aggression and his fast fists. He wound up losing a lot of fights, though, due to the fact that he was usually outnumbered. The brave bullies at Balmoral High School seemed to only run in packs back in John's day.

While working behind the scenes as a stagehand on the high school's version of "No, No, Nannette," John made a fateful error.

The theater department had used the large gymnasium floor to stretch out the 200-foot-long stage lighting system for testing. John's stagehand job was also being performed in the gym. He was to unfurl and paint the flammable cotton material used to recreate stage clouds.

In a tragic case of "you got peanut butter on my chocolate/ you got chocolate on my peanut butter," the cotton material was placed too close to the hot stage lights. The gym took only an hour to burn to the ground, and his nickname "Sparky" was born.

John's dad, Bernie, took his last breath ten years after his mother died, dropping face first in the patchy weeds of the backyard while prepping the Weber cooker for a lonely July evening cookout.

John's older brother was long gone by that time, now living in the neighboring town of Crystal Lake and wanting nothing more to do with John or the house he grew up in.

John always tried pushing thoughts of his family away, but they always circled back. They were unavoidable. John didn't like admitting to it these days, but he desperately missed the family members he tried to avoid in his youth.

CHAPTER

- 3 -

John, on his riding mower, made the final turn for his last swath of tall grass, completed the job and rolled away, passing by a large monument placed in front of the beautiful recreation building at the park.

On the monument there was a plaque with the inscription: "At this site on November 27, 1934, FBI Inspector Samuel C. Frowley and Special Agent Herbert G. Collins, both of the Chicago FBI office, attempted to apprehend then Public Enemy #1 "Baby Face" Nelson. A running gun battle ensued along Illinois Highway 14, which ended near the entrance to North Side Park. Both Inspector Frowley and Special Agent Collins were mortally wounded, as was Nelson."

John had stood in front of that plaque many times, reading and looking out at the park-scape. The modern recreation building (complete with an indoor pool) to one side, the octopus-like, tubular slides of the new water park to the other and a McDonald's positioned at the entrance off of Route 14.

He imagined what the place had looked like that November day back in 1934 when "Baby Face" Nelson took his last breath. He tried and tried to envision the blowing snow covering the expanse of frozen grass, bare trees and a gray, low-cloud ceiling of a 1934 Balmoral. But it never came to him.

It was, however, the place where he decided to wear the see-through plastic baby-face mask for his side job. It was his darkly comedic homage to the murderer mentioned on the plaque.

John would often wonder if other Goth kids had grown up to view the world as he did, through jaundiced eyes. Or maybe they'd sold out and joined the rest of the world, chasing the joys of McMansion ownership. He thought to himself, "I'm a Goth - all grown up," and smiled.

As he made his way toward the McDonald's, he saw a flash of violent activity out of the corner of his eye. The smartass teenager, a kid John knew as Staley, who had just called him Sparky, was throwing punches at a smaller boy about 15. The boy, Danny, wearing shabby clothing, was doing his best to deflect the blows. But the smartass Staley was bigger and stronger and Danny was taking some real punishment.

John didn't exactly tackle Staley, but the forearm shiver he applied knocked the larger teen to the ground. When he scrambled to his feet ready to fight, he was shocked to see that it was John who had supplied the quick jab.

"Fuck you, Sparky. This is between me and that asshole."

John turned to Danny and asked, "Are you okay?"

Danny backed away, wiping blood from his nose and said, "Fuck both of you."

"Not cool, Sparky. Not cool at all, man."

John gave "the look," and Staley smartly exited toward the town's center.

John got back on his mower, made a turn toward following Danny, but stopped. He didn't need any undo notice on him now, especially with his robbery scheme working out so well. John watched as Danny made his way toward the tree line and disappeared from view.

This wasn't the first time that John had noticed Danny. He'd seen him before, usually lurking around the edges of the park, strolling or sitting alone, and looking troubled. Danny wasn't a Goth kid like John once was. He didn't deck himself out in the dark attire, but he looked raggedy as if living on the streets.

John, of all people, knew the signs of a teen in need of help, and Danny fit the bill. Even in the upscale area where John lived, there were still a few families in need.

A couple of times in the past, he had thought about stopping his mower and introducing himself to the 15-year-old kid, but he always pulled up short of actually doing that.

"He'd think I was a perv, or something," John thought to himself.

The car horn startled him from his daydream.

John took in a sharp breath as one of Balmoral's finest, Officer Jimmy, a no-nonsense cop, slowly rolled up in his black and white police cruiser, giving John a suspicious once-over.

"How's it going?"

"Hot one today, huh?" said John.

John surveyed the new police cruiser that Jimmy was operating and added, "You drive Chargers now, huh? More power I hear."

Jimmy shook his head, turned the steering wheel and said, "Quit blowing off those fucking firecrackers. We got people calling us."

"I didn't do that," John lied.

He had actually lit three or four just a half hour before Jimmy showed up. John's favorite pastime was lighting cherry bombs and tossing them onto the train tracks that bordered the park. He especially enjoyed doing that when a train was actually passing.

The railroad company in question had recently taken to increasing the number of freight trains rolling down their cross-country rails. Sleepy little Balmoral saw a 1,000 percent increase in freight train traffic in the past two years.

This never sat well with John. The trains, sometimes screaming through town every hour on the hour, would wake him up in the middle of the night. The winter months were the most awful because the sound-deadening, lush foliage of the area was laid bare. The distinctive, train rumble would travel for a mile or so through the town in the colder months.

Jimmy said, "Get a real job," and drove off.

John watched as he drove away and then looked back to where Danny had made his way through the tree line, but the kid was gone.

John hopped back onto his riding mower, replaced his earbuds and chugged his way toward his house. It was time to "re-Vike" as he called it. The sudden burst of adrenaline from breaking up the kid fight had washed all the soothing effects of the previous 500 mg of Vicodin away. He revved the mower's engine as he headed for home.

At the center of town, John waited on his growling riding mower for a green light at the intersection of Main Street and Balmoral Road. He daydreamed about what another hit of Vicodin would do for his afternoon, how it would make the dreariness of his existence seem hopeful and warm by comparison.

He sat there and admired the beauty of his little burg. Balmoral was not like other suburbs in the Chicago area. It had the usual, small-town, main intersection with quaint shops and diners. There was also an old style movie theater designed by the renowned architect Alfredo Iannelo, some finer eateries, and the commuter train tracks running along the edge of downtown.

But things changed when you got just outside the immediate area of the one square mile town.

Many years ago, the original planners of the township wrote an ordinance that called for five-acre lots (minimum) outside of the town proper. What this ordinance accomplished was making it so John's little village would stand alone. It was a true small town and an island among other suburbs.

There was no suburban sprawl that butted up against and tainted the quaint, little burg. Residents were, of course, very proud of this fact. You could hear them from time to time at Dink's Diner disparaging other nearby suburbs for their crowded ugliness.

Because of this law, wealthy Chicago residents, many of whom were horse enthusiasts, began building estates just outside the Balmoral village limits. Soon the area became known as "Chicago's horse country."

Mega malls never quite made it to the area because the picturesque horse paddocks stopped them in their tracks. Sure, you could head ten miles south to the enormous Woodfield Mall or the up-market Arboretum at Route 59 and I90 or the Deer Park Towne Centre four miles to the east, for all of your mall-shopping needs. But where John and his neighbors lived, it was a sort of modern-day Mayberry, right there on the outskirts of the massive Chicago area.

Another car horn shook John from his daydream, and he noticed that the light had turned green. John waved a "sorry" to the car whose driver had alerted him, and his hand stopped mid-wave. Jimmy the cop stared back at John through the windshield of his police car. John hit the accelerator, and the riding mower inched along through the intersection.

Riding south along Balmoral Road, nearing Coleridge Avenue, John made a right and headed toward his home in the 200 block.

About halfway down the first block, he spotted Danny crossing at the intersection of Coleridge and Lilly. The kid must have used the pedestrian cut-through, where the railroad tracks bordered the park, to get there so quickly. John tried to make the mower go faster, but there was just not enough juice left in the small Briggs & Stratton motor. He pulled the mower to the curb, shut it off and made a run after Danny.

He caught up to the teenager about a block away at Lilly and Trussell; the young man was not happy at all to see John approaching. But he stopped walking anyway.

"What do you want?"

John looked the raggedly dressed kid up and down and measured his words carefully. He didn't want to scare him off because he was truly concerned for his welfare.

"You don't have to talk to me, I get that. But I understand more shit about your life than you probably know."

With a quick, "Fuck off," Danny spun and walked away.

Instead of following, though, John offered, "My folks weren't there for me, either. They thought they were. At least my mom did…until she died. But they weren't."

Danny stopped and without turning, flipped John the bird and kept walking.

John added, "So, we're cool?"

That got a real laugh out of the retreating Danny. He stopped, turned and flipped the bird again, this time accompanied by a smirk. John's dry humor hit its mark.

Danny continued along his way and added, "You're kind of a douche, man."

John watched as Danny turned onto Trussell and headed back toward downtown. The kid, now smiling, looked back over his shoulder as he made his way along the sidewalk and that made John happy.

CHAPTER
- 4 -

The back of the house on Coleridge wasn't as nearly egg-stained as the front. An errant egg or two launched from the sidewalk out front made its way over to the backside of the roof, but not many. John figured that the brave souls who egged the front didn't quite have the cajones to step into the rear yard to even out their handiwork.

The dilapidated, detached garage at his house was occupied by a powder blue 1979 Chevy station wagon and a slew of half ripped apart mechanical projects. There was a push mower with the motor missing, a gutted, old toaster oven, and a few crappy computers in various stages of dismemberment.

Upon further inspection, though, one could see that they weren't fix-it projects at all, but the beginnings of junk-based sculptures. John had been tinkering with bits and pieces of the metal components of the discarded refuse and making them into foot-high renditions of a singular person sitting in a chair. They all sort of looked the same, a man sitting alone looking off in the distance. There were actually five finished pieces, all about the same size each produced from soldering pieces of metal together.

Above the sculpture projects, inside a wall-mounted cabinet, sat the 9mm pistol and a stack of plastic baby-face masks that John had purchased at a costume store in a strip mall.

John rode the mower into the open spot next to the station wagon and shut it down. He dismounted and entered his house.

The inside of the Coleridge house hadn't seen a design team since the late 80's. Neon, sage green, desaturated maroon, and a country apple and rooster motif that his mother deemed "classy," ruled the day. The place was tiny, consisting of a living room, kitchen, one bathroom and two bedrooms.

Everywhere you looked, apples and roosters fought it out for your attention. Mary was especially fond of wallpaper borders high on the wall where they met the ceilings. The particle board and honey-finished, veneer furniture was the cheap icing on the apple and rooster motif cake.

It wasn't that John couldn't afford to update the house. He had the money. The cash in the bank didn't come from pulling off robberies, either.

After his father, Bernie, rag dolled face-first into the backyard, John inherited not only the free and clear home itself, but also a life insurance policy worth $500,000. That was quite a sum for a 23-year-old man to possess. John was stunned to learn that his older brother didn't want any portion of the house or the insurance money. He truly wanted nothing to do with anything Mary and Bernie possessed, and that included John.

At 23, John may have been a tad antisocial, but he wasn't stupid. He quickly taught himself how to play the stock market in the boom years of the 1990's. He was a very aggressive player in the market, turning that initial $500,000 into what John deemed a "tidy sum" over the course of ten years.

Like his town of Balmoral, John had lost some worth during the downward spiral of the late 2000's, but he also had diversified by that time, making sure his investments weren't exposed to be weighted into any one space. He was not afraid to completely pull funds and place them into less risky bonds and CDs when necessary.

While most were losing their asses, John was down only 3.5 percent across his investment portfolio - quite a feat for the "Goth all grown-up."

Right now, though, the 37-year-old John Caul was preparing some scrambled eggs in the kitchen, while being eyeballed by one-dimensional roosters and flipping through the Yellow Pages. He was allowing his fingers to do the initial legwork for his next side job.

CHAPTER

- 5 -

The dark green Saturn with the "Coexist" bumper sticker parked at the low-rent apartment complex next to the closed pizza place was perfect.

It was 2 a.m. and the streetlights of the apartment complex weren't in operating order. That was the cherry on top. Saturn's steering columns were easy to crack for some reason. Maybe it was the imported materials that GM used. John wasn't sure, but he was happy to see the Saturn parked only one-half mile away from his next intended target which was a busy diner called the Athenian near the intersection of Route 12 and Dundee Road in nearby Paladin. Or maybe it was in Arlington Heights. All the suburbs blended together in this area.

It really didn't matter because John knew from scouting the restaurant for the past few hours that it was open 24 hours a day and that business was brisk. Best of all, he'd not seen one Paladin (or Arlington Heights or whatever) cop car pull into the lot.

Most everyone knows that cops have their favorite places to eat. One cop tells the next, and so on and so forth and soon enough, the establishment has a reputation as a "cop place."

The Athenian was not a cop place for one simple reason: Jason, the burly Greek, immigrant owner, who felt at home working the night shift, didn't like to serve his food for free. And uniformed police officers are especially fond of free food.

Jason enjoyed working the night shift from time to time since those were the hours that he was used to keeping when he was a young man growing up in Alimos, Greece. He was also stoked that it was a Saturday night.

From time to time, especially when a drunken customer got out of hand, it gave him a reason to use the skill set he had acquired in his former career as muscle for a low-level Greek crime boss named Akakios.

Although obviously Greek, the crime boss Akakios had a flair for all things French. He constantly went on and on about being reincarnated from French aristocracy or some bullshit. He mostly wore frilly French-made suits and silk socks. In the mid-80's, he went all "Miami Vice" with his French attire, looking as much as he possibly could like a 280-pound version of Crockett.

Akakios' crew didn't believe a word of the Frenchie crap he spewed, but they played along with the boss because he paid well. He also had a penchant for killing anyone who pissed him off, which was more often than his victims were fond of.

And in a bit of false advertising on his parents' part, the name Akakios meant "not evil" in Greek. When Akakios was whacked by one of his competitors as he was banging a 19-year-old imported French prostitute on his 65th birthday, the younger version of Jason saw the writing on the wall. He had several family members in the Chicago area and decided to move stateside.

Now 50 and sporting a frame of 5' 10" and 240 pounds of fat-covered muscle, Jason was a barrel-chested, pussy cat – at least until he was provoked.

He knew all about the Baby Face Robber, as the media had dubbed John. Jason was impressed by the crook's prowess, pulling off armed robberies all in the same 15-mile radius without getting caught or even having a decent description of him relayed to the public. Simple in its design, the plastic, baby face mask was that good at hiding the user's identity.

Jason watched the news on the TV positioned behind the counter, smiled, and thought, "This guy would be a rich man in Greece, with their willy-nilly police protection and corruption. They'd never catch him."

But the Paladin version of Jason had a business to protect.

With Paladin's finest avoiding his restaurant since he lacked the cop charity gene, he had, just the week before, gone to the Sebela's sporting goods store in Hoffman Estates and purchased a military-style, short barreled 12 gauge, pump-action shotgun. It sat, loaded and ready to go, in the corner of his cramped restaurant office.

John left his Chevy wagon parked a block from where he had snagged the Saturn. As he pulled into the Athenian's parking lot, surveying the clientele in the booths along the windows and the few patrons sitting at the long counter, he noticed one, simple fact. The vast majority of the 12 or so customers inside seemed drunk. It was Saturday, but that could be trouble if one of the drunks decided to use their beer muscles to be a hero.

There was work to do, and a Fourth of July celebration to save, so he moved forward with his plan.

Idling the Saturn with its lights off next to the dark, green-colored dumpster where it would blend in, John made his way to the front door with the mask on top of his head, secured by the thin, elastic strap. He scanned for any visible security cameras and saw none. In three, precise moves, he pulled the mask down over his face, extracted the 9mm from his waistband, and yanked the door open.

Jason saw it coming, too, but he froze.

He was more accustomed to the hand-to-hand violence of his youthful Greece muscle days, or with the occasional unruly customer here at the Athenian, just not the gun-toting sort. The 9mm threw him off his game just long enough for John to get the advantage.

John swung the 9mm, aiming directly at Jason's nose, and stepped in close but not near enough so that the burly Greek could grab the pistol.

"All the cash in a to-go box. Now."

The drunk man at the counter closest to John, with a forkful of blueberry pancakes hovering near his quivering mouth, looked confused. When his alcohol-soaked synapses finally grasped the situation, he puked on the floor.

John said, "Shit. Hurry up!"

Jason eyed his office door where the shotgun sat all snug in the corner.

John said, "Who's back there?"

Jason shook his head and said in broken English, "Not no one."

Something was boiling up in Jason, though, a feeling he hadn't had in about 25 years. It was the overwhelming sensation that he needed to hurt someone. John noticed the sea change in Jason's demeanor and backed up a step.

When Jason didn't grab a to-go box, and he didn't open the register, and he didn't comply by filling said to-go box with the proceeds from the brimming register, John did something he'd not done in any of the other robberies.

He fired a shot into the ceiling.

All the other patrons hit the floor, screaming and crying, and begging for their lives. Instantly, without prompting, they even started tossing their wallets and wads of cash out into the open area of the restaurant floor. Even the skinny waitress tossed her wadded roll of tip money into the growing pile.

John said, "I don't want your money. I want his."

The gunshot didn't frighten Jason at all. It only made him madder.

He grabbed the paper money from the register, slapped it into a to-go box and said, "You think you're Dillinger or some shit, huh?"

"Keep filling it."

John noticed that the spent 9mm cartridge was lying on the floor next to the drunk man's ear.

"Give me that."

But the drunk man didn't understand what John was asking.

"The shell casing."

"Don't shoot me, dude. Please…"

John motioned for him to hurry, and the drunk man fumbled around trying to grasp the 9mm shell casing. He finally grabbed hold and handed it up to John.

Jason's eyes bore into John.

He said, "I find you, you know. I've done this sort of thing, you know. I do it to you. Not scared of you one bit."

"Come on, come on."

"I take that baby face off and kill you. Slowly."

John believed him.

Jason finished filling the to-go box, snapped it closed and slid it across the counter. John grabbed it up and made his exit.

Outside the Athenian, as casually as he could, John strolled to the idling Saturn, opened the door, and happened to turn back toward the street. Jason charged from the front doors of his business, shotgun in hand. John scrambled to get inside the vehicle and put it in gear. Jason wracked a round into the 12 gauge shotgun and took aim, but John was already peeling away. Just as the Saturn passed within 20 feet of Jason, he pulled the trigger, but nothing happened.

He had forgotten to take the safety off.

"Pidiksu! Pidiksu!" (Greek for "Fuck you! Fuck you!")

The Saturn accelerated out onto Dundee Road and made its escape. John pulled the mask off his face as he pushed the gas pedal to the floor.

Jason's stubby fingers finally found the safety and snicked it off, but the Saturn was already out of view.

After parking the Saturn, John made his way on foot through the darkness to where his Chevy wagon was parked. The Balmoral Fourth of July celebration was soon to be richer for his efforts.

The Saturn sat empty in the very same spot it was previously taken from, as if it had never been taken in the first place.

By John's estimation and with his careful perusal of his town's official government web site, complete with detailed past and projected village budget numbers plainly displayed, he needed to raise a shitload of more money to make the celebration match the previous years. He feared that he may not be able to pull off his plan in time.

He never anonymously dropped off at the municipal building the exact amount he stole. He knew that if he did, the cops would probably figure out that the Baby Face Robber and the "Save the Fourth Money-Dropper," were one in the same. He mixed up the amounts and sometimes delayed the drop a few days after the robbery. It seemed to be working out so far.

But right at this very moment, John was more than ready to drop the money in the municipal building lobby, head home to "re-Vike," and settle down for a little shut-eye.

CHAPTER
- 6 -

The ten customers inside Dink's Diner was a hodgepodge of retirees and the hard-core unemployed. This was Balmoral, the sixth richest zip code for an area of its size in the United States, but people were still hurting. Maybe the occupants weren't smarting enough not to afford a comforting breakfast of basted eggs, fluffy pancakes and Kona coffee, but still.

John, bleary-eyed from the night before, sat at the corner table nearest the bathroom, the last table Lou, the Greek immigrant owner, would even consider giving to any of his customers, even the ones he didn't like. The table was usually the place where Lou stored the dirty dishes when business was brisk and the dishwasher was getting backed up.

John's table had no silverware or coffee cup setups. It was up to him to get his own fork, knife and spoon. He also had to fill his own coffee cup from the Bunn coffee maker nearest the kitchen pass-through on the back of the eight-seat counter.

Lou and the 80-year-old Emil commiserated in the booth nearest the front door. Both of the men took suspicious glances at John from time to time.

As John got his own cup of coffee, he nodded a good morning to the dreadlock-wearing cook, Larry, who smiled and said, "What'll it be, John?"

Larry felt a kinship with John. Larry was a wise and compassionate man for his 21 years on earth. He also knew a thing or two about being on the wrong side of bullies.

He grew up in Wilmette on Chicago's North Shore as the son of a printing press operator who had purchased a broken-down piece of property in the midst of one of the wealthiest neighborhoods in America. His dad made an incredibly brilliant financial move by purchasing the house, which was originally built in 1910, and fixing it up. Larry's dad tastefully renovated the home all on his own, tripling its value in just a few years' time. He sold that initial house and purchased two more, living in and rehabbing both, while Larry attended high school.

But Larry's dad never took into account what it would be like for his only child to live among the country-club set as essentially a sensitive and artistic, blue-collar black kid.

Larry didn't receive a brand-new Mercedes on his 16th birthday like several of his classmates had. He was okay with that. He didn't take European vacations in the summer or hit the slopes of Vail at Christmastime each year, either. But he did excel at his Trier High School art classes enough to be awarded a minor scholarship to the Art Institute of Chicago.

Painting just wasn't enough for Larry, though, so he quit school. He wanted instant, artistic gratification. He wanted people to enjoy his work now, without him waiting to grow old and die to finally be noticed. That led him to a career as a tagger in the Bucktown neighborhood of Chicago.

He was arrested for spray painting what he considered to be some of his best work, a rendition of Godzilla tit-fucking a stacked female Mothra, on the side of a yuppie couple's brand-new garage. While recuperating after being beaten by some gangbangers whose turf he'd wandered into a few days after the arrest, Larry decided to try cooking instead.

Cooking was artistry. It was instant. You immediately saw how your work turned out and if it pleased the critics sitting at the tables in the front of the house.

And the best part was that he got paid money to do it.

Larry was a master at presentation, even in tiny Dink's Diner. Presentation was all about color, texture and height. His plates were beautiful, and the compliments he received buoyed him even more than the $10 an hour ever would.

John said, "Surprise me."

Larry knew that meant corn beefed hash, poached eggs, home fries and rye toast. As he began preparing John's order, the front door opened.

John dropped the full cup of hot coffee on the floor as Jason, the owner of the Athenian, stepped into the diner.

Lou jumped to his feet. He tried to greet Jason and berate John at the same time.

"What the hell, man?"

"I got it, Lou. I got it. Sorry," said John as he located the waiting mop and bucket in the corner near the bathroom door. He carefully picked up the broken bits of coffee cup and eyeballed Jason as Lou hugged him.

Wait, Lou hugged him?

John was confused for a split second. The spark of realization soon flooded his brain, though. Lou and Jason were brothers. They had nearly the same frame, the same dead eyes. They had the same salt-and-pepper, curly hair.

Jason took a seat with Lou and Emil, and now all three of the men peered John's way. Jason seemed to take a special interest in John. He turned and began telling his brother a story.

John couldn't quite make out what they were saying in their hushed tones, but he knew that Jason had to be relaying what had happened to him the night before. Lou tried to calm his brother by patting the back of his hand, but Jason was in no mood. And he kept glancing at John.

John, as quickly as he could, finished picking up the bits of broken cup, mopped the floor and replaced the bucket and mop into the corner.

"There you go, John."

Larry slid the beautiful plate of food up onto the pass-through and John took it and his seat as fast as he could. He tried not to pay any attention to the large, Greek men eyeballing him and dug into his incredibly delicious food.

Larry stepped from the kitchen with a cup of coffee in his hand and took a seat across from John.

"Thanks, Larry. Perfect, as usual."

"Did you notice?"

This was a game Larry liked to play with John called, "guess the new ingredient." John smiled, chewed and closed his eyes.

"Cumin?"

"Fuck you, man. Nice. You know your herbs."

Larry studied John and said, "Why is it that you're always so mellow? I mean nothing seems to bother you. These assholes talking their shit when you come in and you just sit there and take it."

John would have loved to tell Larry all about how the Hydrocodone and Paracetamol combination in the Vicodin he had ingested an hour ago was washing its way over his brain, rounding the hard edges off of the animate, inanimate, and emotional, but what he said was this.

"I do yoga."

"Fuck you, yoga."

John flicked his eyes to where Lou and Jason sat and said, "What's going on?"

"Lou's little bro got tagged for a grand or so last night. That baby dude--"

"Baby Face Robber got him? Shit."

John was acting cool, but trying to eat his food and get as much info from Larry as he could before making a quick exit.

"He get a description this time?"

John noticed Jason really staring hard at him, not wavering

42

at all.

"Nah. But they'll get that fucker soon enough."

"I'd bet on it," said John.

Larry nodded toward the counter.

"Lou's got a cannon under there just in case," he said and then added, "but I've noticed the son of a bitch never tags places in Balmoral. Strange, huh? Probably afraid of Jimmy."

"Jimmy the cop's a scary guy."

Larry sipped from his cup and said, "Know what I'd do if that baby fucker-"

"Baby face."

"-came in here?"

"No, what?"

"I'd applaud him, man, what do you think? Thumbing his nose at the man all this time. In this area, too. Cops are fucking pissed that they can't nab the dude."

Jason, staring at him with cold eyes, stood up, and John nearly choked on his food. The Greek began stepping toward John and Larry. John, without making any quick motions, slid his free hand over and grasped the butter knife. But Jason walked right past him and the cook and entered the bathroom.

John began shoveling the food down his gullet when movement out the front windows and across the street stopped him.

Amy, the receptionist from the dentist's office he robbed in Lake Zurich, was stepping from the dry cleaners with a piece of paper in her hand.

John watched her for a brief moment, not remembering where he'd seen her before, until it finally dawned on him. This version of Amy looked more determined than terrified. This version of Amy was well-dressed and displayed a pleasant demeanor.

John had to get closer. He had to see if she was okay. It didn't hurt that she was a stunningly beautiful woman, either.

He reached into his pocket, pulled a $20 out and tossed it on the table.

Larry said, "You okay, John?"

"I'm good. Hey, I just remembered that I have to be somewhere."

"What's on for today?"

"Thinking about heading up to Wisconsin."

"Nice, man. Fishing?"

"Yeah, maybe," said John.

John got up just as Jason walked from the bathroom. After they bumped into one another, Jason and John stood nearly nose-to-nose. The angry Greek man sized up John. John smiled, nodded and left the diner.

Out on Balmoral Road, he caught up with Amy as she waited at the light to cross Main Street. He didn't speak, but noticed that the piece of paper she was holding was what he had expected it to be, a job application.

The walk sign illuminated, and they both began crossing the street, maybe John a little too close for her comfort. She nervously looked over her shoulder, but John stared straight ahead and continued along.

John had heard through the Vike vine that the dentist closed up shop in Lake Zurich right after the robbery. He had been depleted of all of his cash and inventory of white, little, football-shaped pills.

With the dentist never practicing any real dentistry, he was forced to immediately abandon the dingy offices and head to greener pastures. That, of course, meant Amy was out of a job.

The somewhere the dentist ended up was Naperville, Illinois.

A year after the robbery at the crappy office in Lake Zurich, the dentist was killed in a freak accident while working in his new office. Maybe "freak accident" wasn't being totally accurate. And "working" was debatable as well.

The dentist had found a new backer, a no-necked guy named Brick who lived on the West Side of Chicago. Brick had provided the start-up funds and initial inventory needed for the dentist to get his new Vicodin operation under way.

Brick knew that a dentist's office would be the perfect front to work a sizeable operation with "patients" coming and going - no one would be the wiser. But when the dentist was caught skimming a larger share from the agreed upon profit participation plan, Brick did something he'd never done before in such a situation.

He called the cops - the Naperville police to be more specific. He knew that the dentist wasn't stupid enough to give the cops his name. He just wanted to put a scare into him. Hell, if the cops shut him down, so what? He'd find some other floundering dental professional to work with. There were plenty to choose from.

When a detective from NPD arrived at the dentist's office to question him about the anonymous tip, the dentist overreacted by barricading himself into his crappy, new office on Ogden Avenue. He quickly announced that he was armed and that he'd taken a patient as a hostage.

The Naperville SWAT team shut down all the traffic on busy Ogden Avenue and had the office surrounded in less than 30 minutes. A negotiator began talks with the dentist shortly after the SWAT team was in place.

After a couple of go-rounds of communications between the dentist and the SWAT negotiator, and offers of Domino's Pizza and sodas in exchange for the negotiator's chance to speak with the hostage, the police determined that the dentist didn't have a hostage after all. Well, that and the dentist's receptionist, a no-nonsense, Haitian woman that Brick had hired for him named Bert, telling them that there never were any real patients in the office - not ever.

The SWAT negotiator and his team were also confused by the lack of effort by the dentist to communicate with the outside world.

Usually barricaded individuals wanted to speak by phone, or in person (which was never allowed) to loved ones and friends. But the dentist made no such requests after his phone system was rerouted to the negotiator sitting in the command vehicle a block away. The equipment used to pick up any cell phone conversations was silent as well.

The lack of communications on the dentist's part made the SWAT leader believe that the dentist was depressed and a suicide risk. A plan of attack was set in motion.

The dentist wasn't a suicide risk. He was just lonely. He didn't have any family or real friends who he could or even wanted to talk to. So he decided to sit in the examining chair and relax. The comfortable and ergonomic nature of the chair, coupled with the lack of incessant traffic noise on Ogden due to it being shut down, was enough to gently coax the dentist into a restful, napping state.

The breach began when the SWAT leader fired a tear gas canister through the side window of the dental office. Unfortunately, in a morbid, Rube Goldberg-like scenario, the canister made a direct hit on one of the fluorescent light fixtures in the ceiling, ricocheted off a wall-mounted poster of a molar, continued along its zigzag course and knocked the top off a small oxygen tank sitting next to the examining chair the dentist was reclining in.

The dentist, having awoken to the sound of shuffling feet near the building, watched the whole thing play out as if in slow motion.

The four-inch-long canister smashed through the window glass and demolished the light fixture above. Sparks fell everywhere. Next, the canister smacked into the molar poster with a thud, and the dentist heard the nearly instantaneous, pinging sound of metal-on-metal (canister to oxygen tank valve), and the sickening, hissing sound of escaping, flammable gas.

He was able to determine his fate in a nanosecond.

"Fuck me..."

The explosion didn't level the building, but the oxygen tank, ignited by the sparking, broken light fixture overhead, acted like a three-foot-tall hand grenade.

The dentist left behind a nearly empty ranch-style home in Schaumburg, a Porsche 944, a new Land Rover, with the sticker still on the window, a 26-foot Boston Whaler (with trailer), and a lawn service crew wondering who was going to pay them for the past month's work on his property.

Perturbed, Amy finally stopped in the middle of the street.

John nodded and said, "Nice day, huh?"

"Are you following me?"

John continued on, passing her. They made it to the other side of the street and John turned left.

"I'm sorry. Did I frighten you?"

Amy said, "Sorry. God, I'm sorry. I don't want to seem... never mind. Have a good one."

Amy continued north on Balmoral; John, west on Main. But John quickly stopped and backtracked. He watched as Amy crossed the railroad tracks and stepped into the BMW dealership. There was a "Help Wanted" sign posted in the front window.

CHAPTER
- 7 -

The surface of Lake Geneva was like glass and boat traffic was at 50 percent.

"An anomaly," thought John, as he maneuvered the 26-foot Crestliner from the private dock in Fontana, Wisconsin, where he had stolen it, to the public docks in the town of Lake Geneva proper.

Lake Geneva was usually a freshwater, maritime, drunken madhouse this time of year. Even on a weekday, boats would normally choke the lake. "A guy could get used to this calm," thought John.

The boat, named "The 'Nort' Side," was obviously owned by a wealthy Chicagoan. The Cubs and Bears stickers plastered everywhere on the inside compartments confirmed it. And like most Chicagoans, the owners must have believed that nothing bad ever happened in Wisconsin. That's why they left the keys in the ignition. John felt comfort in counting on human nature.

The area had been Chicagoland's playground for over a century. The beautiful lake, rolling hills, quaint shops, hotels, spas and restaurants filled the R & R bill. And it was all only a

90-minute drive away.

John had been on boat rides here in the past. White-knuckle affairs when he was a kid with his dad and his dad's best friend, George, a lawyer who specialized in setting up trust funds. George was a Zen master at operating his 18-foot bass boat, unafraid of the real dangers of the overcrowded lake. John could remember the insane, crisscrossing mancuvers that George had to make just to keep from getting run over by the larger, faster boats.

John hadn't planned on taking a boat this close to his final destination, a high-end resort on the northeast part of the lake just outside the town of Lake Geneva. It was such a clear and sunny day, though.

He caught a glimpse of the calm lake as he passed the Abbey Resort on Highway 67 and knew his plans would have to change. He was going to have to steal a car somewhere in the area anyway. He could always leave "The 'Nort' Side" at the docks, steal a car nearby, do his work, and circle back to the Abbey Resort to pick up his Chevy wagon. It was too beautiful a day for rigidity.

He couldn't find a Saturn to steal this time, so the plain white, 1995 Chevy van tucked into the back of the Denny's parking lot would have to do. He parked it in the side lot of the cheap "no-tell" motel next to the high-end resort's property and trekked through a tree line, the baby face mask and 9mm pistol hidden under the cheap Wal-Mart windbreaker that he zipped up to his neck.

CHAPTER
- 8 -

John was in a fantastic mood - nonchalantly driving the Chevy wagon south on Highway 14 on his way back to his home in Balmoral.

He replayed the robbery of the upscale hotel over and over in his head. He chuckled to himself recounting his stroll directly through the crowded and ornate lobby, where no one paid him a lick of attention.

The lack of response on any potential witness' part was due to the large, wine tasting in progress. Free wine and cheese was the catnip John needed to allow his plan to go off without a hitch.

Last month's Travel + Leisure magazine for the Balmoral area had an article about this resort in particular and how popular their midweek, mid-afternoon, free wine and cheese tastings were. A lobby full of tipsy people stuffing their faces with complimentary, Wisconsin cheese was the perfect cover for his crime.

Hitting a place in Lake Geneva was not in his initial plan to rob only breakfast restaurants in the suburbs surrounding Balmoral. Well, taking down the dentist wasn't in his plans, either, or the spa, for that matter. That was kismet. But after hearing on the local news just that morning, that suburban police departments were possibly starting a Baby Face Robber task force, he had a change of mind. Maybe striking in Lake Geneva was just the thing to confuse the police. Or maybe it was just the Vicodin clouding his thought process.

And okay, he had to admit to himself that robbing the dentist's office was probably more about the Vikes than the cash. He could live with that.

Slowing for traffic in Harvard, Illinois, he imagined the way the 22-year-old, male, desk clerk giggled when he saw the mask back at the Lake Geneva hotel, but how he soon lost his smirk when the cheap 9mm came into view.

John sat up straighter, prouder, thinking of the exchange of money from cash drawers to his plastic bag and his departure that took less than one minute. He smiled at the memory of the leisurely walk back out of the lobby and through the tree line to his awaiting getaway van.

Sure, the $5,750 in the bag under the passenger seat and ultimately the saving of the celebration was his goal, but John couldn't help thinking, "Damn, I'm good at this."

There was a larger reason that he was in such a pleasant mood, though. It was the main reason that made it difficult for him to shake his dopey grin.

It was the never ending, circular thoughts of Amy playing through his mind. He tried to push them away, but they'd come right back -- the way she looked back at him as they crossed the street earlier, how her attractively snug clothing fit her backside. He obviously didn't know her, but he could tell the instant she confronted him in that crosswalk back in town, that she was the girl for him.

When they first met at the dentist's office she was sort of a mess, but who wouldn't be with some dude pointing a gun at you?

He had a good feeling that she was a strong individual.

She seemed like someone who could fend for herself. He loved strong and intelligent women, although he had never actually dated one. Most of the women John had been with only wanted to have a good time. There was nothing ever serious about the relationships, nothing permanent. And for John that was okay, until now.

Getting the money was fantastic, but landing a woman like Amy could be life-changing.

CHAPTER

- 9 -

Amy Bowling, the former receptionist at the dentist's office, wasn't originally from the area.

A strikingly beautiful, country girl, with dark, wavy hair, she'd grown up in hardscrabble Jackson, Kentucky, in the heart of Breathitt County. She was the second oldest child, and eldest girl, in a family of nine siblings (four girls and five boys). Amy was also an unwitting, second mother to her seven younger brothers and sisters.

At 18, she escaped not only the oppressive poverty of rural Eastern Kentucky, but the forced motherhood her parents required of her.

Illegal pot-growing was, and still is, one of the top-producing cash crops in Kentucky. While her parents were gone for days at a time tending the pot plants that they had placed on lush, public property hillsides all around the county, Amy had to provide in some way for the rest of her family. This involved working two legitimate jobs, one as a cashier at the Piggly-Wiggly, and another dealing soft-serve at the Dairy Queen.

She graduated near the top of her class at Breathitt County

High School, but with her parents trekking all over the county in the only family car, higher-paying jobs were just not within walking distance of her home.

Her older brother, Dwayne, was of no help at all because he was doing a ten to 20-year stint in the Kentucky State Pen for felonious assault on a police officer.

Dwayne had been completely caught up in the family business, and when a Kentucky State trooper named Deaton stumbled upon Dwayne tending to a cache of pot plants off the side of Highway 15 near Frozen Lake, they had a come to Jesus moment.

Dwayne had a talent for shooting. If he hadn't been drummed out of the Marine Corps two years into a four-year stint for knocking out a loud-mouthed sergeant, he may have taken a more positive turn in life - maybe, but probably not.

The several marksmanship awards he'd received in his two years with the Corps worked against Deaton in the worst way. The state trooper took two rounds to the chest. Fortunately, his ballistic vest saved his life. However, the round he took to his right kneecap was career-ending.

The trooper, hampered with the low ground and losing blood at an alarming rate, managed to sink two rounds into Dwayne's right quadriceps and one bullet into his left shoulder. Over 100 shots were fired between the two men before backup arrived for Deaton and Dwayne ran out of ammo.

Breathitt County, where Amy grew up, was also known as "Bloody Breathitt County" for the number of violent feuds that erupted there over the years, starting just after the Civil War. The last known, official feudal killing happened in the 1970's.

Breathitt County's feudal violence was nothing like the romanticized and mostly media-made, Hatfield & McCoy version. It wasn't violence over perceived slights and defending family honor. The troubles were more akin to the brutal mob violence of 1930's Chicago. It was about money, power and the control of illegal activities.

Now it's Oxycontin, pot and Meth, but 80 years ago, the Breathitt County moonshine business was booming in the days of Capone.

When the Chicago mobster himself sent a delegation of sophisticated, city mobsters to negotiate away the lucrative, moonshine enterprise from the local yokels, it didn't work out for the city slickers. As one tobacco-chewing local at the time put it, "They found dead I-talians hanging from the trees up and down Highway 15." Capone cut his losses and looked elsewhere for future, business opportunities.

Breathitt County's own took care of Breathitt County.

A few years' back, a documentary film crew from one of the myriad cable channels was run out of town because some of the locals didn't like the questions they were asking. The documentary crew was inadvertently stirring up violent outbreaks all around Jackson by dredging up old wounds.

An 18-year-old Amy Bowling took a Greyhound bus north after her mother finally came to her senses, got out of the family business and began taking care of her own children. Amy saw her opening to freedom and quickly took flight.

She found herself a cheap room to rent just outside of Cincinnati and a job working as a housekeeper for a wealthy family in the suburb of Indian Hill. It took some effort getting from the old house where she rented the room to the affluent suburb, transferring buses twice, but it was ultimately worth the effort.

She met a young man from the Chicago area who was visiting her employer's son. His name was S. Winston Fletcher (the S. standing for Stanley). His closest friends affectionately named him DB (short for douche bag), but Amy called him Winston. He was studying business with her employer's son at Miami University in Oxford, Ohio.

Winston was a smooth-talking, handsome and well-kept man of 21. His parents owned a construction company based in Lake Zurich, and Winston, their only child, was in line to take over the business.

At first, Amy couldn't understand why such a cultured young man was taking a liking to her. After Winston invited her to a college party in Oxford and witnessing the jealous reactions she was getting from the snippy and entitled sorority sisters in attendance, Amy's confidence began to blossom.

The boys back in Jackson would tell her that she was pretty and would constantly try to get her alone in parked cars on desolate roads out in the county, but she thought they were just bored and not really interested in her. She had younger siblings to take care of first. The awkward pawing in parked cars wasn't important to her. It was annoying.

There was a reason Amy graduated near the top of her class at Breathitt High. Unlike the goobers back home, when the pretty, rich boy Winston began pawing, she had an awakening. She knew whether she ended up with Winston or not, that she'd never have to live in a place like Jackson ever again.

She made a concerted and successful effort to lose her Kentucky drawl and blend into the Chicago area culture she moved to as a young bride just six months later. But as homage to her roots, she kept her maiden name.

The majority of the past 14 years were an incredible, uphill, roller-coaster ride for Amy.

They lived in a five-bedroom, French provincial home in the exclusive Chicago suburb of Deer Park. Every year, Winston traded in her last year's model, two-door Mercedes coupe for the latest version. They enjoyed vacations in Europe and a condo on South Carolina's posh Kiawah Island. She partook in weekly spa treatments and had a live-in maid.

The only price she had to pay was the loneliness.

Winston was gone a lot. Working, he'd say. In neighboring Lake Zurich, the family business was construction. They did mostly foundation work for projects all around the country in the poured cement trade. It was lucrative work for Winston, whose father retired from the company shortly after Winston graduated college.

The father moved to Costa Rica one year later after Winston's mother died in an apparent accident, a 20-story fall, while visiting friends at their high-rise condo in Miami.

Then two years ago, the FBI made their first call on the French provincial home in Deer Park. Winston was out of town on business at the time.

Amy told the agents that he was in Las Vegas, bidding on a new hotel construction contract. But they had photos of Winston and what looked like a younger version of Amy, canoodling on a beach in the Bahamas. The photos were taken just that morning.

The FBI agents weren't stupid. They knew the best way to get to Winston was by pissing off his wife sitting back in frigid Illinois. So while he was getting a nice tan and his pipes cleaned on a white, sandy beach, Amy was being grilled in her own living room.

It was the first time that Amy had heard of her father-in-law being referred to as "Big Anton." She always knew him from the rare visits as Tony Fletcher. He seemed like a kindly, little, gray-haired man, not the monster the FBI was making him out to be. They said as a teenager, he was a hired killer, and as an older man, a mob boss. She couldn't wrap her head around the idea that her father-in-law's real name was Anthony Capelli. It all seemed like nonsense to Amy.

"Wait, are you saying, Winston?" she asked.

"Wake up, Bowling," the larger of the two agents said, knowing her general background and that she kept her maiden name. "You know what's going on now. You may want to consider moving out of here before it gets ugly for you, ma'am. You should be grateful there are no children involved."

The agent, Hugh Rogers, had grown up in London, Kentucky, and knew that he could talk the talk with Amy. Although she was sitting in a 7,500-square-foot home in Deer Park, she was still Jackson, Kentucky at heart. He never threatened her with arrest because he truly believed, especially after the way her face went completely without color at the mention of the Fletcher-Capelli family affairs, that she was an innocent.

After learning of the FBI's visit, Winston never did come home from the Bahamas. He joined his father in Costa Rica, where they both lived a carefree existence in a lush compound with a quarter mile's worth of beachfront.

Costa Rica has an extradition treaty with the U.S. but the Fletcher-Capelli's were very adept at greasing the right palms. They'd never set foot on American soil again.

Six months after that first visit by the FBI, Amy, with no means of support, was forced to move from the French provincial home. By that time, the grass was so long from neglect, the property looked like an abandoned home. The Mercedes was gone, as well.

She stood in the driveway studying the house after loading the last of her designer clothes into the back of a waiting taxi and thought, "Who am I kidding? I should've known."

She moved into the basement of her friend Lori's house in Lake Zurich. They'd met at Fletcher company parties and picnics over the years. Lori and her husband, Jerry, a project manager at Winston's company, who also lost his job in the whole FBI-Winston fiasco, were very understanding and supportive friends.

Amy hadn't lost her looks but her confidence was shot. It took her a year or more to simply begin a job search. Jerry was able to land another job soon after the company went under and had no problem helping to support the woman he knew had nothing to do with his former company's demise.

The very first job offered to her, she took. It was at a dingy dentist's office in Lake Zurich near Routes 12 and 22. So close that she could walk to the office on good weather days.

She lasted two weeks before the place was robbed by some idiot wearing a see-through, baby face mask.

The robbery turned out to be a blessing for Amy. First, the dental practice was a sham. She knew it from day one. No patient would stay for more than five minutes at a time. And from growing up in the Oxy capital of the world, she knew the signs of opiate abuse. It didn't take a Betty Ford Clinic therapist to figure it out, either.

For eight hours a day, Amy would survey a waiting room occupied by people of all stripes with sunken and sleepy eyes, people who would constantly be scratching their arms and legs. She knew immediately that she was a smiley face, medical scrub-wearing window dressing for an illegal, drug-selling operation.

The most annoying part of the job, though, was the ruthless and constant sexual advances by the dentist. She could handle herself and keep him at bay, but she was afraid that she'd wind up knocking the shit out of him and losing the $150 cash he gave her at the end of each workday.

On the day of the robbery, with the waiting room unusually empty, the dentist had cornered her behind the front counter. He kept trying to touch her hair and whisper in her ear. The dentist didn't know how close he was to owning a pair of swollen testicles. Amy was quickly approaching the boiling point of frustration and anger when the door opened.

"The money and all the Vikes you have," the robber said.

To an outside observer, they would think that Amy's terrified expression was due to the robbery in progress, but they would be wrong. She was relieved.

The sense that she was off the hook bubbled up and made her cry and her face contort. She realized that she needed to stand up for herself, like she did 14 years earlier when she left Jackson. She knew that no one would take care of her other than herself. She realized that she had lost herself inside the big house in Deer Park and that she wasn't being true to herself all these years.

The gun in her face didn't scare her at all. She was ecstatic knowing that she had found her rudder once again.

That's why she ran.

She knew the guy in the mask wasn't going to shoot her. She'd seen guys like him on several occasions back in Jackson.

"He's all talk and no action. This guy would be on the ground with a blank stare back home," she thought to herself.

She ran.

Neither the dentist nor the robber could see it, but she was smiling ear to ear as she hit the door and sprinted down Route 22 toward her friend Lori's house.

She never went to the cops, she didn't even tell Lori and Jerry what happened, she just took to advancing her life of independence with more purpose. She knew she'd have to start from the bottom and work her way up from there. The idea excited her to no end.

She wanted to manage a business. It didn't matter to her if it was a dry cleaners or an automobile showroom, she wanted to take her shot at guiding a business toward growth and prosperity. It was her chance to shine.

CHAPTER

- 10 -

Tyler mopped the floor at the Athenian before the dinner rush. His concentration wasn't on the job at hand, though. He was more interested in keeping a close eye on Jason.

His dark, curly hair and expressive eyes were those of a little boy but, at 6'3" and 265 pounds of solid muscle, Tyler was a man-child. He was also an unusually sensitive kid of 17. Maybe not so much when he was chasing down opposing quarterbacks as a defensive lineman for the Maine High School football team in Park Ridge, though. He was a straight-A student and recently had been awarded a full academic and football scholarship to Boston College. But now he was troubled like never before. He fought back tears while witnessing his father Jason battle his own feelings of inadequacy in the wake of the Baby Face Robber incident.

Tyler had never seen his father so depressed before. Jason's head and heart weren't in his business or family life any longer. Instead of being out front greeting and enjoying playful banter with his customers, he sat in his tiny office and allowed the waitresses to run the show.

At home Tyler stood by as his father watched inane cooking and home improvement shows on television, something he'd never done in the past. Jason was usually vibrant and always conjuring up a family activity to do, from miniature golf, to seeing a movie, to whatever.

Now Jason was an empty shell.

But after hearing his father weep through his closed bedroom door in their Park Ridge home the prior evening, Tyler knew he had to do something. That's why he withdrew the $4,500 from his savings account and hired a private investigator he found on Craig's List.

The private investigator, Enright, a disgraced former Evanston police officer, was happy to take the case. Enright was, at one time, an aggressive cop. After getting his ass kicked while trying to stop a garage burglary in progress on the west side of Evanston his rookie year on the force, he took to instruction in the Israeli special forces method of Krav Maga fighting.

Enright trained at a dojo in Skokie for a few years and became an excellent student of the martial art. Krav Maga or "contact combat" in Hebrew is a brutal form of self-defense. The fighting style had been invented by a Czechoslovakian Jew and former boxer in the 1930's who was sick and tired of getting beaten by the Nazis who would wreak havoc on his small village.

The Czech's hostile invention incorporated nearly every style of fighting the world over in what would become one of the most effective defensive-aggressive, hand-to-hand combat techniques known to man.

Enright had been kicked off the police force for using his Krav Maga skills to shake down drug dealers of their cash to supplement his own kid's college fund. He was good at what he did.

He was a master at hunting down bad guys. When he found them as a sworn officer of the law, he'd take their money and brutally beat the shit out of them, but that was the dangling carrot he needed to get the job done.

Enright knew that this Tyler kid didn't care about the money, so if there was any robbery proceeds left over when he caught up with the Baby Face Robber it was his to keep. That plus the $4,500 would make for a good month.

They met in a blue and orange-colored Franklin Finch Ice Cream/Dip Doughnuts franchise building. The playful, colorful and boxy buildings had been popping up all across the Midwest of late. In blind taste testing done by the Chicago Tribune's food critics, the ice cream won hands down – the doughnuts, however, were subpar. This ice cream and doughnut shop was located in Des Plaines. Or was it Mt. Prospect?

"I can do shit the cops can't. I'll find him. You got the money?"

Tyler handed Enright the cash out in the open. "Come on, kid? Think." The private investigator quickly stuffed it into his pants pocket.

"Sorry. I didn't know," said Tyler apologetically. He added, "Don't hurt the dude, okay? And don't get the real cops involved, either. Not until I meet the Baby Face Robber face-to-face first, okay?"

"Sure, makes no difference to me," said Enright. "I'll corral him and then he's all yours."

"And no one will know?" asked Tyler.

"Probably better they don't. It'll be just between you and me," said Enright.

"When you find him, I'm going to-"

"Whoa! Plausible deniability, kid. Don't tell me any more, okay? I still have some ethics, you know?"

"Huh? Oh, right," said Tyler.

But Enright knew what Tyler was going to do. As a cop he'd seen it all before in kids Tyler's age - teens who had been dissed and were bent on revenge.

Tyler added, "After you get him for me, I'll pay you $10,000 more. Is that cool? It'll clean me out, but it'll be worth it."

Enright feigned a nonchalant attitude, but this bonus was a

complete surprise. He was thinking "Ya-fucking-hoo!" But what he said was, "Yeah, sounds fair."

After their meeting Enright went to his grayish, blue-colored, one-bedroom apartment on Northwest Highway in the Jefferson Park neighborhood of Chicago and did a simple Google search. He read all about Tyler, the star athlete and straight-A student.

"Boston College? No shit…," thought Enright, "And his dad owns a successful restaurant in the burbs. I wonder what Tyler's old man would pay to keep this all quiet. His kid hiring someone to find the son of a bitch who robbed him, so he can kill him?"

At the Athenian, Tyler finished mopping the floor and rolled the bucket past his father's open office door. Jason sat at his desk looking blankly at the nearest wall.

The 12 gauge shotgun was no longer resting in the corner of the room.

CHAPTER
- 11 -

Jimmy the cop was a nervous wreck.

This was an unusual state for the normally confident 42-year-old man. Dressed in his civvies, he parked his personal car in back of the Balmoral police department and armed only with a handful of number two pencils, he made his way inside.

Back in 1989, he'd seen and done things in the Marine Corps that would make most people go weak in the knees.

As a highly effective and aggressive 21-year-old sergeant, he helped to guide his men against Panamanian Defense Forces (PDF) in "Operation Just Cause." Taking point after hitting the beach, Jimmy and the men in his charge made quick work of the shoddily trained PDF on their home turf of Panama City.

For his efforts, Jimmy was chosen as one of the Marines who escorted a handcuffed Manuel Noriega to a waiting C-130 transport plane. His photo was seen the world over, and it helped him to the land his current position.

Thinking back to the .223 rounds zipping over his head as he returned withering fire while lying in the wet beach sand didn't make him sweat, but the idea of again failing this fucking lieutenant's test he was about to take certainly did. It was eating him up inside.

This was his fourth attempt at the test. He was a man of action, running headlong into enemy fire while taking out seven PDF soldiers' singlehandedly, but shit, this goddamned test.

He was always able to prove himself physically throughout his life - as a hard hitting free safety for Balmoral High's football team, a state qualifier at 189 pounds on the wrestling team, a trained killer in the Marine Corps or as a no-nonsense cop, but he never had success in the classroom. Book learning was his Achilles heel. It wasn't that he was stupid. Quite the opposite was true. He was street-smart, just academically incurious.

As he passed the age of 40, though, his thought process began changing. His body would only hold out for so long, so he hit the books. He knew that if he wanted to stay in the job he loved, that he needed to change his stripes – from sergeant to lieutenant. As a commander, he would be behind a desk more often than in the field.

The bump in pay would help, too, especially with two daughters attending Northwestern University. They were on academic scholarships thanks to their mother, and Jimmy's ex-wife, being a brilliant woman herself, but there were still expenses to take care of.

Jimmy couldn't just fire a few rounds of his department issue Glock .40 caliber pistol into the test and be done with it because that would be too easy. He had to ace this fucker so there was no doubt that he should be named the next "Lute."

After flunking the test so many times before, Jimmy wanted to prove to his brethren that he wasn't an idiot, although they had ungraciously tagged him with the nickname, "Flunky," behind his back.

"All set, Flunk-, ah, Jimmy?" asked the chief, holding the paper packet containing the test.

Jimmy, sitting at the desk in the empty sally port of the police department, couldn't even speak. He gulped, nodded and tapped the desk where he wanted the chief to place the exam.

"You have two hours. You can start - now," said the chief with a knowing smile.

Jimmy didn't like the way the chief was looking at him, his expression a mix of torment and ridicule. As Jimmy was about to spout a smartass remark of his own, something deep in the recesses of his mind calmed him. It was an inner voice that he had heard as he hit the beach in Panama City. It was a voice that he hadn't heard in over 20 years. It warmed him and gave him confidence and comfort. The voice is what got him safely off that beach all those years ago as the PDF .223 rounds zipped over his head. What the voice said was this.

"I'm gonna light these assholes up now so I can fuck their wives tonight."

Jimmy giggled at the thought.

"What's so funny?"

"I've been meaning to ask you, how's your wife doing these days, chief?"

The Chief lost his smirk, shook his head and left.

Jimmy hunched over the exam, readied his number two pencil and began the test in earnest.

CHAPTER
- 12 -

John sat on a barstool furthest from the door, sipped his drink and admired what the new owners had done with the place.

Once a Hooters-like sports bar, recently it had been reopened as a tastefully decorated Irish pub with lots of dark wood and brass accents. The large windows facing Main Street and the beautifully renovated train station were a nice addition to the decor. The drink and food prices were higher, but the clientele was better. The absence of Hooters-like girls will do that.

Anytime John could enjoy himself in a place like this without having to prove his might to some drunken 22-year-old with beer muscles was a win-win in his estimation.

He liked eating his dinner out before the main crush of passengers disembarked from the arriving rush hour trains. They'd jam places like this along the tracks, meeting their significant others or simply sitting at the bar drowning their sorrows and avoiding their significant others at home a few blocks away.

The bartender delivered an order of shepherd's pie to John, "There you go, Sparky. Want another Sprite?"

John placed a hand over his drink and began digging into his dinner when the front door opened, and Amy walked inside.

She had that look of purpose on her face that John found so appealing. As she surveyed the place, John looked down into his delicious shepherd's pie and took a bite.

"Is the owner around?" she asked the bartender.

"The manager is. Hold on a sec," he said as he stepped into a back office.

Amy thought to herself, "Of course they have a manager. Maybe there's something else?"

There were only five customers in the place at the time, and John knew he needed to play this cool or--

"Hey, I know you," said Amy.

John, a forkful of shepherd's pie hovering near his mouth, faked confusion, "You do?"

"The other day? I made an ass of myself as we were crossing the street."

"Sure, okay," said John.

She nervously tapped her fingers on the bar awaiting the manager's arrival and said, "Doing some job hunting."

"Yeah? How's it going?"

Amy shook her head and said, "Sorry, don't mean to bother you while you're eating."

Contrition – the opening John was looking for.

"No problem at all. Would you like to join me while you wait?"

Amy thought to herself, "This is a nice looking man. He's polite, too. His hair's a mess, but it adds character."

"Okay," she said.

John extended his hand, and they shook as she sat on the stool next to his, "John Caul."

"Amy Bowling. Nice to meet you, John. How's the food?"

"You've never been here before?" he asked.

"Nah, but it looks like a nice place. I saw where they just opened a few weeks ago and was checking to see if they needed any help. Maybe a manager. Too bad the bartender there said he was getting the manager, so…"

John sipped his drink and said, "That your game, restaurant management?"

"Um," Amy sized John up and thought to herself, what the hell. To shed the past you need to own it and allow it to fall away as quickly as possible. "No, I haven't worked a real job in about 15 years. My husband left me. Actually the FBI's snooping around made him leave me."

"Oh, I didn't mean to pry…"

"No, this is good, John. Unloading this crap to a total stranger is sort of freeing if that makes any sense."

"I guess…"

"Can I help you?" said the manager, a burly man in his thirties, as he stepped through the office doorway.

As a smiling Amy engaged the manager in conversation, John noticed someone watching him through the front window. It was a shabbily dressed, shadow figure.

To John, Danny had no discernable expression but his eyes were eerily locked onto him. The kid finally turned and disappeared from view.

Danny was sort of confused by it all. It was because the dude was like 40-fricking-years-old, but still, Danny thought John was awesome.

John was at the top of Danny's "cool" list, especially so after he poked fun at himself following the fight with that asswipe, Staley, at the park. Danny wanted to get to know John, maybe hang with him, but didn't know the correct protocol in engaging older dudes in conversation.

Even though he'd only lived in the area for a year, he had heard the stories of John and how he had burned the school gym down back in the old days. Danny thought the idea of burning down the school gym, hell, any part of a school, was amazing.

Danny's avocation, and his first love, though, was of making up and telling stories.

The stories he told were always about real people in his life like his parents, a neighbor or a classmate. Although the stories seemed factual, they were always nearly completely fabricated. They were wicked ditties woven in the mind of a troubled, 15-year-old boy.

One story he conjured, and that was circulating at the high school at the moment, was about Staley and how he had screwed one of the older lunch ladies at school. The story was untrue, but Danny was a master of his craft. Details mattered. He always researched his story enough to make the scenario plausible in the audience's mind.

He was a master of the three-act structure, taking his young and unsophisticated audiences on a dramatic, roller-coaster ride.

Yes, the lunch lady was in her late fifties but she was built like a mo-fo. Everyone at school knew that Staley was a tit man. Shit, he'd tell you point blank himself, if gently prodded. The students also were aware that the lunch lady in question was overly friendly with the male students. The particular story that Danny crafted had Staley and the stacked lunch lady doing it in the walk-in cooler on a row of chicken nugget boxes. It had just enough ring of truth that it worked, and it quickly got the anti-Staley ball rolling at school.

The burly teen, Staley, didn't know what hit him or where the story originated, until he heard Danny himself, that little prick of a raconteur, spouting off the story to a couple of cheerleaders in the cafeteria. Danny was quicker on his feet and got away – that day.

Danny was sort of an asshole and usually kept people at arm's length, but he liked it that way. Keeping people in check allowed him to live within his own head, free of the outside world's static.

He had a feeling that maybe he and John were kindred spirits and that the older dude was sort of a contrarian like he was.

Danny was gleefully aware that people in town thought he was from a bad home and that he was neglected.

"But they didn't know shit," he'd tell himself. "It's just another fucking story, Sheeple. Wake the fuck up."

Actually Danny had been raised, up until a year ago, in the posh San Mateo Hills of the San Francisco Bay area. His mother, Sharon, a highly regarded clinical psychologist, and his father, Donald, an executive with an international beverage company, were relocated to the Balmoral area by Donald's employer.

Danny was a seemingly well-adjusted kid until two years ago when his parents welcomed a surprise baby boy named Joseph. His little bro was a cute and fun little dude, but Danny found that all of the attention usually aimed his way quickly evaporated as soon as the baby came into the home.

He began acting out soon after.

His decline into semi-juvenile delinquency started small. One day, he skateboarded at a high rate of speed past the multi-million dollar homes on steep Parrott Drive in San Mateo, screaming and yelling obscenities at the wealthy residents who got in his way. But, it soon escalated to where Danny was hanging with the fringe elements of a dangerous gang near Central Park in downtown San Mateo, working as an unofficial lookout-in-training for weed slingers.

That's when Danny began his storytelling avocation and the reason the gangbangers-in-training liked having him as an unofficial lookout. He was a well-dressed suburban kid who could tell any patrol officer a plausible story thus keeping the heat off the drug dealers.

His mother, Sharon, would normally know how to handle issues like a "kid from a good home gone wrong." She'd dealt with children in the same type of situation in her practice. But those patients weren't her son. Unfortunately, she was emotionally handcuffed and ineffective.

When Danny's dad, Donald, was given the chance to relocate with his employer, the family moved as quickly east as they could, hoping the fresh start and Balmoral would be the tonic needed to snap Danny out of his juvenile delinquent funk.

Except for the storytelling, the move had seemed to work. But, Danny was becoming restless again, dressing like a homeless person, and seeking out more and more dangerous activities, like pissing off a 210-pound, 17-year-old kid named Staley.

Danny stepped back toward the front windows of the Irish pub and took another peek inside. The old dude was speaking again with the pretty lady in the fashionable pantsuit. They seemed to be hitting it off and that made Danny do something he'd not done in a while – sport a sincere smile.

The idea came to him right there. He wanted to know how this guy John ticked, what he did every day, who he knew, where he lived. There was only one way to gather that information.

Danny would have to follow John every chance he could get.

Inside the Irish pub, Amy ordered the shepherd's pie and a beer.

As they waited for her meal to arrive, she gave the "nickel tour" of her life and everything she'd been up against to this point (Kentucky, Winston, the FBI and the dentist). She felt that she could open up to John, who seemed to be such an excellent listener.

The Vikes in John's blood system were wearing off. Except for the constant scratching of his limbs, he seemed engaged. A couple of times he tried, when she wasn't looking, to shake his head from side to side to snap out of his drug-induced malaise. He wanted very badly, or so he thought, to get to know this beautiful woman.

"No, that house was in Deer Park off of Long Grove Road and Buckeye. The one where I'm living now is in Lake Zurich near Routes 12 and 22 in back of the grocery store and the Italian beef place. Lori and Jerry have been so supportive, but I have to get out of their basement soon. The rents here are so high, though, don't you think?"

"I wouldn't know. I've owned my house outright since I inherited it."

"Oh, so both of your parents…?"

"Yeah, it's okay," said John.

The bartender stepped from the back with Amy's dinner. Amy

picked up her fork and dug a trough into the mashed potatoes on top releasing a pocket of steam.

A sad thought came to him. "It's my brother who I miss," said John.

"That's horrible. So all your family members are gone?"

John scratched at his arm and said, "No, not my brother." Her confused expression edged him along, "He's still around. We just don't talk."

She waved a hand over the opening in her shepherd's pie and nodded to his scratching.

"What's wrong?"

He looked down and lied, "Dry skin, sorry." And then he stopped scratching.

"So I'm hoping the BMW dealership I was telling you about works out. That would be an exciting job, I think. Seeing people negotiating over big ticket purchases. I'd like that."

He had this beautiful woman sitting right next to him. It was what he wanted, a chance with her, but all he could think was, "Shit, it's time to re-Vike." He took a deep breath, willing a brief moment of sobriety into his brain, but his eyes rolled up into their sockets instead.

Amy instantly knew that she made a mistake in conversing with John. He was starting to act like he's drunk, yet he's not drinking.

"Shit…you're a goddamned addict," she whispered.

She'd seen this type of thing back home and, more recently, at the dentist's office. What the hell was wrong with the world that people thought they needed to run and hide in the delusional state that downers brought on? Well, probably a stupid question but still, there was a lot of this shit going on around here. And this was a fancy neighborhood, too.

"I have to run," she said as she got to her feet and collected her purse.

John was lost in thought for just a second and that was the cementing moment she needed. She turned to walk away.

"Huh? What? Where are you going?"

She stopped, dug into her purse and pulled out a $20, tossed it on the bar and headed for the door.

She said, "I don't need any more shit in my life at the moment."

John, defeated, knew exactly what she meant. It was just a matter of time before someone noticed that he had a problem.

"Shit…"

CHAPTER
- 13 -

The other massive homes with their manicured lawns and in-ground pools were situated all around the French provincial. But Amy's old residence, sporting two-foot high grass, a broken, picture window in front and weeds growing through the cracks in the blacktop driveway, was the pimple on the ass of this wonderful street.

In exasperation, he again checked the numbers on the return address portion of the crumpled and stained envelope. They matched the numbers on the house, just not the image he had in his mind. As he adjusted the backpack on his shoulder, a voice startled him.

"Can I help you, sir?"

Dwayne turned and tried to act as cool and calm as he could.

"Shit, the Deer Park police are stealthy fuckers," he thought. Dwayne didn't hear the cop car's engine or the officer approaching on foot. Or maybe he was just too caught up in the disappointment of learning that his sister, Amy, no longer lived in the house.

"I'm good, man. Just trying to visit my sister. Amy Bowling.

You know her?"

The Deer Park cop, Officer Hynek, was an 18" necked, no-nonsense bull of a man. "Step over to my vehicle, sir. Let me have that," he said as he pulled the backpack away from Dwayne.

Dwayne, having dealt with the screws in the Kentucky State Pen for the past 15 years or so, knew to comply in a peaceful manner.

Dwayne said, "Nice neighborhood, huh?"

Officer Hynek took the envelope from Dwayne's hand and read it. He saw the Kentucky State Penitentiary address.

"For your safety, sir, I'm going to ask you to put your hands behind your back."

"Sure. I feel safe already," said Dwayne as the cop clicked the handcuffs on him.

Officer Hynek grabbed Dwayne by the arm and walked him to the back door of the police car. "Just make yourself comfortable and we'll sort this all out at the station, okay?"

"Sounds good to me, officer. You wouldn't happen to have any sandwiches there, would you? Sort of hungry. You know, you being all worried about my comfort and all."

Officer Hynek pushed Dwayne into the back seat and slammed the door closed. Dwayne looked at Amy's former residence and was saddened to think what may have happened to her and the life she created for herself.

But, he'd find out what happened.

Now that he was a free man, he had a lot of time to figure things out.

CHAPTER
- 14 -

She knew something was wrong a week ago.

It was a mother's intuition. She watched as her talkative and intelligent son became nearly mute in their Park Ridge home. She had asked repeatedly what was bothering him, but backed off her questioning yesterday when he broke down in tears and holed up in his bedroom for the rest of the day.

Now Rita, a beautiful and solidly built woman of Greek descent, Jason's wife, and Tyler's mom, could wait no longer. She had to know what was going on. She tried subtle, but subtle wasn't going to cut it any longer.

Rita was raised as the youngest child and only daughter in a family of five from the Sauganash neighborhood on the North Side of Chicago. Her father, Alex, a humorless man, owned and operated a small trucking company based in Niles. Her mother lived in the quiet desperation of an immigrant woman wanting all that was America, but fearful of what her disapproving husband would think of her.

Rita was treated like a princess by her mother, ignored by her father and played a sort of whipping horse to her older brothers.

She grew to be a princess with a punch of her own, though. A trait her older brothers grew to appreciate.

She rarely backed down from a fight, especially when it came to protecting her two sons. Other mothers and kids in her current neighborhood figured that out fairly quickly, especially 11 years earlier when two older neighbor boys tried to bully a six-year-old Tyler.

Rita didn't go after the boys, both just ten at the time. She went after the kids' mothers, both at the same time. No punches were thrown, but the bullies' mothers got the message and got their kids in line. And ever since that episode, the neighbors would rather stay on Rita's good side.

"Mommy, what's wrong," said little Christopher, her five-year-old son.

Rita near tears herself said, "Nothing, peanut. Go and wash up. I'll make you some lunch, okay?"

As Christopher happily hopped away humming to himself, Rita bit her lip. She couldn't wait any longer. She marched from the kitchen, up the stairs and walked right into Tyler's room without knocking.

Tyler, lying on the floor with his iPod earbuds in, sat bolt upright, "Mom?"

But Tyler knew the look Rita was giving him. He knew she was going to figure this all out and get to the bottom of it all.

She said, "It's time, Ty. Spill it!" And he did.

CHAPTER
- 15 -

"This is the last one," he said to himself as he popped 500 mg of Vicodin into his mouth and swallowed it down with a cold chug of bottled water. He knew to land someone like Amy that he was going to have to cease his drug-taking ways.

"How the hell did the habit get so out of control?" he said out loud as he maneuvered the old Chevy wagon through the group of houses near Routes 12 and 22 in Lake Zurich.

But he knew exactly how his addiction started.

He was prescribed one pill a day at bedtime so he could sleep, but a few years down the road, the urge to take more was too much to ignore. He went in search of illegal sources to supplement the 30 pills he got from Walgreens on the 15th of every month.

It wasn't difficult to find someone willing to help him out, either. Nor was the introduction to the Twitter-based Vike vine. There was an odd camaraderie among Vicodin addicts, and they tended to look out for one another. Naturally, it cost money to have this type of friendship, but he never went without the little, white, football-shaped pills for very long.

His intense back and hip pain wasn't the first symptom that he experienced.

It started innocuously enough when his left big toe became numb eight years prior. Soon, his left leg up to the knee was pretty much feeling free. But the numbness, oddly enough, was coupled with pain - shooting nerve pain - the worst kind of pain in John's opinion.

It all soon intensified, becoming a buzzing and gnawing pain that was, most times, too much to endure. The numbness and pain soon migrated over to his right big toe, leg, both of his hands and part of his face. The back and hip pain kicked in soon after.

There were bouts of disorienting vertigo, especially when he was vaulted into bright sunshine from a darkened building or the intense, humid heat of a summer day. He sort of lost track of the when and where of it all, but he finally went to a neurologist who, after intense testing over the course of a few years' time, confirmed what John had suspected was going on all along.

He had multiple sclerosis.

He remembered the day the neurologist displayed the images of his brain and spine from his MRI. It looked as if someone had dipped a small brush into paint and splattered his brain and spinal column with little white dots. Multiple sclerosis translates to "many scars," and John had them.

His doctor had wanted to get John started on a regimen of injectable medications that could possibly help to slow down the progression of the disease, but John refused. He had done his homework and decided that the medications the doctor wanted him to take were hit-and-miss with their effectiveness. He would rather alleviate the pain and deal with the inevitable progression on his own terms.

There was only one other person he knew, other than his doctor, that was aware of his diagnosis. But if others saw him stumbling or in pain, he'd make up a plausible excuse of a sore knee or something similar and go about his day. And really, he knew that no one would care if Sparky had an inflammatory disease or not.

And so far, the MS hadn't affected his robbery activities. Although his feet were now completely numb, he had conditioned himself to jog without injuring his ankles or feet. He could still pull off a quick burst of speed when needed, like at the French-named spa in Deer Park. But that burst would only last for about 50 yards until the lack of control would take over again.

He also kept in shape by riding a recumbent bike that was set up in his basement and by watching his diet fairly closely (with the exception of the corned beef hash and eggs at Dink's Diner). If need be, he was ready to take flight if things went to shit, maybe not at a full gallop, but at a brisk jog.

He had actually absorbed what Amy was saying back at the Irish pub. Although it took a nap and a quick memory run-through right after waking up to remember it all.

She had said that the house was located behind the grocery store and Italian beef place at Routes 12 and 22, but he was having no luck in locating it. Who was he kidding? It was a shot in the dark anyway. He didn't know what kind of car she drove, and all the homes in the area looked nearly identical. Two stories tall, boxy, all painted either tan or slightly different shades of tan, with the two-car, attached garage on either the right or the left side of the property.

"Hold on. She said her other house was off of Long Grove Road," he said aloud as he pulled a U-turn and sped out of the neighborhood. "There are not as many homes over there... because they're fricking huge."

CHAPTER
- 16 -

When he placed his hand on her knee, she had instantly punched him in the jaw with a left jab, followed by an immediate right to the nose.

As his portly 230 pounds tumbled to the floor, the startled customers and salespeople all looked their way, but Amy wasn't embarrassed. She stood over him like Muhammad Ali ready to knock the son of a bitch out.

"Is that what it takes to get a job here, Mr. James?" she said quite loudly as he tried to get to his feet. "I bet the customers would love to know how you treat perspective employees, huh?" she added in an even louder tone.

Mr. James, a fat little fucker, wiped blood from his left nostril and looked up at Amy with wild and frightened eyes. "You'll need to leave," he said.

"No sir, I will not. Not until you apologize right here on the sales floor. Right here in front of all these people."

"Call the police!"

"That's a fantastic idea. I need to report a sexual assault," she said.

A couple who were right on the verge of purchasing a $75,000 BMW walked out of the dealership in a hurry; the salesman they were dealing with pulled at his own hair.

"Please, just leave," said Mr. James.

But Amy didn't move. She stood with her arms crossed over her chest – waiting.

"Okay, all right. I'm sorry," he said.

"They can't hear you."

"I'm sorry. I'm goddamned sorry! Okay?!"

Amy gathered up her purse and headed for the door. She passed by a saleswoman who stood holding the door for her. The saleswoman and Amy locked eyes.

"Thank you for doing that," said the woman. "I'm right behind you," she added.

Amy nodded and exited the BMW dealership, walking back toward Balmoral's main intersection.

CHAPTER
- 17 -

Sitting at the counter in the Athenian, he couldn't help but notice the depressed mood of the owner, Jason. The short, stocky man had stationed himself in his office and was doing, well, nothing. The poor mope.

He had completed some research on Jason and found out bits and pieces about his past in Greece. It didn't take a genius to figure out that Jason was some sort of mobster back in the old country. But he was clean as an American citizen. "People can change," he thought, with a laugh. "Yeah, sure."

Enright was there trying to get a feel for what his prey, the Baby Face Robber, would know, see and hear as he pulled off his heists. And the pancakes here weren't that bad, either.

Of a secondary nature, if he could get a peek at his next quarry, Jason, that was all the better. By the looks of how brisk business was at this hour in the afternoon, Enright calculated an ask of $50,000 as a starting point to keep his son's murderous activities quiet once the Baby Face Robber business was put to bed. This was a win-win excursion.

He pushed his plate of half-eaten pancakes to the side and

opened a 12 by 10-inch book of maps out on the counter. The page he studied was the portion of the Northwest Chicago suburbs where he sat at the moment.

Little, hand-drawn X's marked the spots of the known robberies. There were two robberies that the public wasn't yet aware of, information he'd gotten from an old cop buddy in Buffalo Grove. Also the Lake Geneva robbery was believed, at this time, to be a copycat crime because it fell way outside the suburban Chicago pattern.

Enright also learned that the suburban police departments were not starting a robbery task force (as the media reported) to help nab the Baby Face Robber. Each department would have to fend for themselves.

Every municipality, even crime spree-ridden areas, felt the pinch of budget cuts.

The Buffalo Grove cop also let Enright in on a little-known detail. The cops didn't care all that much about the robber. The police chiefs of said departments were more interested in making their municipalities more money through traffic and parking citations. Traffic and parking tickets were big business in the suburbs, especially with the economic downturn. There was no profit in catching robbers, just the expense of overtime and a possible trial.

Enright sipped his coffee, picked up his pencil and absently drew a lazy, thin line from one X to the next.

"Holy fuck!"

"We got kids here, mister," said the skinny waitress.

Enright checked his tab - $9.75. He tossed a fifty on the counter and said, "Buy them some fucking earplugs."

He gathered up his map book and exited the establishment. As he charged out the door and headed for his car, he bumped into a muscular man sporting long hair and a tight, Golden Gym tank top. The guy looked as if his favorite vitamin was chewable steroids. His biceps were larger than most people's thighs.

"What the fuck, man?" said the Golden Gym dude.

Enright didn't even acknowledge him as he stepped toward his car that was parked at the rear of the building.

"Hey, I'm talking to you. Hey, fuckwad!" said the Golden Gym dude.

Enright turned just in time to see the Golden Gym dude approaching in an aggressive manner. Enright didn't display any fear at all. In fact, his expression and eyes flattened and a strange calmness overcame him.

The Golden Gym dude leaned forward to give Enright a shove, and that was it. Enright dropped his map book to the ground and in a series of extremely quick and surprisingly athletic moves involving the utilization of his elbows and the heels of his hands, he obliterated the 'roid head.

Enright may have looked like a poorly dressed and paunchy, used car salesman, but he was able to cause some major bodily damage. He could thank his Krav Maga training for making quick work of the larger man.

He left the Golden Gym dude lying on the ground and gasping for breath and continued toward his 13-year-old car. After getting in, he placed the open map book onto the passenger seat and started the engine.

The thin line that the X's helped him create on the map book made an almost perfect circle around Balmoral, Illinois.

CHAPTER
- 18 -

After getting home from a fruitless search for Amy's other home off of Long Grove Road, John had taken two more 500 mg tablets of Vicodin.

There were fewer homes in the area where he had searched, but the odds of locating either Amy or the house she lived in were slim. His plan was to locate the house and question any neighbor he could find to see if they knew Amy's whereabouts.

But the only anomaly he found was a landscaping crew putting the finishing touches on a French provincial home's yard overhaul where a female real estate agent had just placed a for sale sign.

Now allowing the Vicodin to work its warming magic, he could barely read the Dink's Diner menu laid out on the table in front of him. He pushed a stack of dirty dishes to the side of the table and tried to get better light on the menu. It's not that he needed the menu to order; he knew exactly what he wanted to eat. The game he played was trying to see if he could make out the blurry words.

Larry, the cook, knew something was amiss with his buddy.

He delivered John's corned beef hash and eggs himself and took a scat across from him.

"What's going on, man?" asked Larry.

John's eyes had a difficult time focusing on Larry's face but his dreadlocks were quite intriguing to him. He reached out and stroked a few of them.

"Are you okay?" he said as he gently pushed John's hand away.

Larry was no fool. He slid the food closer to John and handed him a fork.

"I'm guessing Vikes or Hillbilly heroin."

John motioned to the stacks of dirty dishes on the table and shrugged. "The dishwasher quit - again," said Larry.

John took a bite of the food, smiled and said, "Cumin!"

"Keep it down, man. Lou's in a shitty mood today."

"Is that not normal?" John asked with a chuckle.

"The regulars are all bent out of shape because they think the town's cancelling the Fourth of July bullshit. If the regulars get their tighty-whiteys in a bundle, Lou does the same. You know that."

Now Larry had John's attention. He said, "What do you mean? I thought someone was giving money to-"

He had said too much.

"How did you know about money rumor? No one talking about that until just today," said Lou in his broken English, sneaking up on Larry and John.

"I heard you talking about it when I came in," John lied. He and Larry shared a quick "let's keep this between the two of us" look.

Lou's jaw muscles worked angrily as he took in the sight of Larry sitting at the table with John. He thought of his next move for just a second or two longer. "You? You fired!"

"What? I didn't do anything. Lou, please," said Larry.

"You and this fuck always talking quiet over here. What you talking about, huh? You make fun of me?"

John said, "Lou, you have it all wrong. Larry loves working for you. He loves working here at Dink's. Don't ask me, ask anyone here."

Larry was frozen in place, near tears, and not even wanting to take a breath. Maybe if he just let things settle without adding anything else to the discussion, everything would be okay, and he could go back to work.

"What the fuck you talking about, Sparky?"

Lou happened to take a look around at the other customers in attendance. All of them looked on with surprised expressions.

Emil said, "He does make good pancakes, Lou."

John said, "Lou, I know you don't like me, but don't take it out on Larry. Shit, do you have an itchy trigger finger, or what?"

Lou worked his jaw muscles again and nodded for Larry to get back to work. Larry got to his feet and made his way to the kitchen without hesitation.

John asked, "What did you hear about the festival?"

"Why should I tell you?" asked Lou.

John shrugged and made a "no problem with me" face and took a bite of food.

"The rumors I hear say money the person leave is not enough. I don't know if I believe any of it."

"That festival has been going on forever," said John. "How much more do they need?" he added, trying to keep cool.

Lou looked as if he wanted to punch John in the head but responded with, "How the fuck do I know? It's rumor. But what can you do about it you piece of worthless shit? Mow lawns until you get cash?"

The rush of anger-induced adrenaline perked John up to a fight or flight level. It was looking like fight until John said, "No need to get personal, Lou." He went back to eating his food and ignored the diner owner, but he knew that his robbery efforts were going for naught and that was extremely troubling.

"I don't like you coming here anymore. This is the last time. No more. Larry, you hear me?" said Lou.

Larry, peering through the kitchen pass-through, nodded and went back to work.

John continued eating and ignored the fuming Lou. He had bigger fish to fry. If the rumors were true, and the festival was actually being cancelled, he was going to have to ramp up his robbery antics. He wasn't sure he had it in him any longer.

His thought process had slowly shifted in the past weeks' time, vacillating between saving the celebration and getting to know the beautiful Amy more intimately. Amy was winning out for his focus of late.

But he had to stop taking the Vikes to even have a chance with her, he knew that. As he shoveled in his last bite, the decision had been made. He was going to quit cold turkey. No more Vicodin for him. He wasn't going to destroy the thousands of pills he had stolen from the dentist's office, which were currently residing in his garage near the cheap 9mm pistol and the baby face masks. He was sure he could use the Vike vine to get rid of them somehow.

Maybe selling the Vikes could help save the celebration? But selling that amount of pills could bring undue notice on him, and that might play havoc on his ultimate plan for himself and the Fourth of July celebration.

And now Amy was muddying the waters – in a good way. He was going to have to stop taking the Vikes, though, that was for sure. The two pills he had popped an hour before were the last that would ever hit his bloodstream.

It was an easy decision to make. The thought of being with her, even with the odds stacked against him of that ever happening, was winning out. As he allowed his breakfast and his anger to settle, there was a gnawing thought in the back of his head, though.

He still had to save the celebration.

Maybe he could have it all? Why not, other people chased their dreams and succeeded every day. Why not him? But he had to stop taking the drugs. That he had to do - starting right now.

CHAPTER
- 19 -

The driver couldn't believe his luck as Jimmy the cop walked back to his Balmoral police car and shut his emergency lights off.

The driver had sped northbound on Balmoral Road, doing 40 in a 25. He drove right through a crosswalk where children were about to enter, continuing north he ran the red light at Balmoral and Main.

Jimmy pulled him over as he crossed the railroad tracks. The driver, a little tipsy due to a three-beer lunch at a day of the week themed restaurant in Hoffman Estates, was on his way to confront his ex-boss after being fired for porn surfing while on company time.

The driver barely had a chance to toss a newspaper over the top of the .38 revolver on the seat next to him, when a smiling Officer Jimmy poked his head through the open, driver's side window and said, "Hiya!"

"Hiya, back…?" said the driver.

"Man, you were booking it, brother. Did you see the kids you almost hit, or the red light you blew?"

The driver was beginning to have flop sweats and his hand

was inching toward the newspaper concealing the .38, when--

"Well, you slow down, sir. Be safe, and have a great day," said Jimmy.

"Huh? Sure…"

The driver took off like a shot, getting out of Balmoral as quickly as he could.

Officer Jimmy got into his car and said to no one, "This is the most beautiful day I think I've ever seen."

He shut down his lights, put the car into gear and slowly drove away, the gentle breeze pouring through his open windows allowing the folded letter on the passenger seat to fully open.

It read: "Congratulations on passing your lieutenant's test." The second line was the kicker, though, "With the retirement next month of Lt. Scharm, you are next in line to take the position."

Jimmy couldn't and, hell, really didn't want to contain his glee, as he slowly drove through the beautiful park on Balmoral's northeast side. The world seemed brighter, and the running and playing children in the park more joy-filled.

All was right with the world.

CHAPTER
- 20 -

He was feeling sick to his stomach as he drove the stolen Saturn away from the gravel company's parking lot.

He had popped so many Vicodin for so long now that he didn't take into consideration what suddenly stopping would do to his body. The symptoms, some launching a surprise attack on his lower intestinal tract, were almost worse than the MS pain. With the DT-like shakes wracking his body, he was barely able to keep the stolen car between the yellow and white stripes of Route 22 in Fox River Grove.

He tried pushing the pain and nausea to the back of his mind and to focus on the task at hand. He imagined what the place he was going to rob looked like. He didn't do any reconnaissance outside of a Google search because, well, he felt like shit and thought that he could improvise this time around.

What could go wrong? He'd gotten pretty damned good at this game, and he needed to trust his instincts.

One thought that kept circling through his mind, though, was his wonderment over how city neighborhoods and small towns became so enamored and prideful of their breakfast restaurants.

Magazine, newspaper articles and TV segments on such breakfast places always seemed to catch his attention, though, so maybe it was simply human nature to be interested and proud.

Morning brought new light, so it could be that the idea of eating a hearty breakfast at such a place did the same for the human psyche. Well, that and most establishments were excellent community meeting centers. Dink's Diner was such a place.

John, outside of wondering what the food would be like, also knew that such businesses were cash cows. So, on top of poking the burgs surrounding Balmoral in the proud-of-their-breakfast-restaurants-and-communities' eye, there was a money-retrieving method to his robbing madness.

He had to try having it all, saving the celebration and getting closer to Amy. Robbing this breakfast joint in Fox River Grove while Vicodin-free would be the first step in achieving his new goal.

As he drove past the front door of the business, he noticed that it was a small place, only about twenty feet from side to side. But there were a lot of cars in the parking lot. Maybe they were there for the other businesses in the small strip mall - a dry cleaners and a nail salon.

He parked in the half full, back parking lot near the dumpster, donned his mask, grabbed his cheap 9mm pistol, adjusted the windbreaker and made his way to the front door.

An old couple in their late eighties was having trouble opening the front door of the restaurant. John quick stepped to the entryway and took control of the situation, allowing the old couple to enter.

"Thanks, kid. Halloween coming early this year?" said the old man, who quickly noticed the gun and added, "You go ahead we don't want to get in your way."

"Thanks," said the shaky John as he strode inside the restaurant and pointed the 9mm at the skinny and food-stained-tie-wearing manager's head.

"All of it in a to-go box. Now," he said calmly.

The manager hesitated because he was completely taken by surprise.

John was so focused on doing his work that he didn't even take a look at where the customers may be. When he did take a glance to his right, he saw an enormous dining area, filled with about a hundred customers – all looking his way.

The twenty-foot wide area he'd seen from the street was simply the waiting area. The majority of the restaurant was built behind the other strip mall businesses.

"Shit," said John to himself.

A woman screamed as loud as she could, the manager hit the floor behind the front counter and the place erupted in pandemonium.

John froze for just a second. "Aw, come on…" He finally turned and hobbled out the front door as fast as he could. The old man held the door for him this time.

As he rounded the building he saw a Fox River Grove police car parked in back of the stolen Saturn. A 24-year-old, male cop with a pimply face was walking a circle around the car and checking it out.

"Shit, shit, shit…"

John turned, passed by the front doors of the restaurant again, where the old man smiled and waved. He pulled the mask up so he could see more clearly as he made his way across the parking lot, dodging and weaving between parked cars and heading for Route 22.

Danny stepped from the driver's door of a large, white Land Rover parked right in front of John. The teen and the robber stood staring at each other for a quick moment.

Anger and hurt brewed in Danny's eyes, though. He finally screamed, "Dude? What the hell, man!? I thought you were cool!"

"Oh, shit, shit, shit," said John as he jogged away, crossed Route 22 and guided himself toward a large field with a dense wall of five-foot high corn rows.

"Police! On the ground! Get on the fucking ground!"

John didn't even look back. He sprinted-jogged-hobbled as quickly as he could toward the wall of cornstalks and disappeared into the thick greenery.

Once out of view of the 24-year-old, Fox River Grove cop, John began zigzagging through the corn rows as he tossed the mask, the gun, and then peeled off the cheap, Wal-Mart windbreaker, tossing that as well.

After making each move, he'd stop for just a moment to see if he could hear the cop's footsteps. After three maneuvers, all was silent. He heard in the distance the cop talking excitedly into his shoulder-mounted radio. He was about 150 feet away and still near the roadway of Route 22. He hadn't really followed John at all, probably adhering to some police protocol of not going it alone.

That was just the police procedure John needed to put as much distance between himself and the Fox River Grove cop as he could.

Now stripped to a white t-shirt and blue jeans, he headed east toward Kelsey Road as quickly as his shaky and numb legs would carry him.

***

Jimmy the cop was at the self-serve car wash on Route 14, taking a break and lazily running some sudsy water over his Balmoral police car when his radio crackled with excited voices.

"We have a robbery in progress. Route 22 near Kelsey Road. White, male suspect wearing a baby face mask, blue windbreaker and blue jeans, armed with a semi-automatic pistol, last seen on foot, east toward Kelsey Road. Any mutual aid officers in the area, please respond," said a female radio voice.

Jimmy looked up at the street sign at the corner where the car wash was located – Route 14 and Kelsey Road. He dropped the hose and spoke into his shoulder-mounted radio, "Balmoral PD unit two is in the area."

The female radio voice responded, "Okay, Balmoral. Thanks.

We only have one officer on the street right now due to training. He's at the scene of the robbery and not in pursuit."

"Copy that," said Jimmy into his radio, as a big shit-eating grin slowly formed on his face. "I'm going to bag this mope," he said to himself. "Then I'm gonna fuck his wife," he added.

***

John, sweating profusely, as much from his withdrawals as the strenuous, impromptu exercise he was partaking in, poked his head out of a row of corn. He looked left and right down Route 22 but saw no police activity.

He thought, "What in the hell was that kid doing in the parking lot back there? And he's in a damned Land Rover!" He shook the thoughts from his mind and focused on his escape. Quickly crossing back over Route 22, John continued east through another cornfield that was located alongside a subdivision.

As he entered the manicured backyard of one of the subdivision homes, a border collie chased him, barking and nipping at his heels. The dog suddenly stopped, though. John turned and caught a glimpse of the dog's electric, fence collar.

"Nice…"

He jogged across Linden Court and through the yard on the opposite side of the street.

***

Jimmy the cop was slowly and silently rolling north on Kelsey Road, the Linden Court subdivision on his left. He had an inkling that if this mope was on foot and heading east, he'd try to blend in here in the subdivisions next to the cornfields.

"We have a caller stating they see the subject on foot northbound on Route 14," said the female voice on his radio. But Jimmy didn't break off his search of Kelsey Road. His gut told him that the perp was heading his way, not west and northbound along Route 14. He was so confident, that he pulled the shotgun out of the rack and placed it across his lap.

***

John bent over and vomited in the backyard of a home that bordered Kelsey Road. He tried to catch his breath and compose himself. He wondered why he didn't hear police sirens everywhere but thought to himself, "They're here. They're just running silent."

He saw a sprinkler working in the next-door neighbor's yard and stepped over, detached the sprinkler from the hose and took a long drink.

John could see that no cars were passing on Kelsey Road. That could mean two things – one, the cops had the road blocked and were searching for him in the area. Or two, it was just not that busy at this time of day.

He stood and considered his options. He could move forward, cross over Kelsey Road and enter the cornfield on the other side, or stay here in the subdivision and meander through the backyards until he could safely make a move east toward his home in Balmoral.

He took a deep breath and hobbled headlong toward Kelsey Road.

***

Jimmy saw the guy in a white t-shirt and blue jeans staggering out of the yard. It looked like he was drenched in sweat. He accelerated and got to within 20 feet of the perp before slamming on his brakes.

John stopped in his tracks and took in the sight of the skidding, soapsuds-covered police car. He didn't raise his hands in surrender because he was just too damned tired. He cocked his head to the side as he read the Balmoral PD insignia on the cop car.

Jimmy, still sitting in the driver's seat, immediately lost his shit-eating grin.

He watched John for a moment before putting the car in reverse and rolling backwards 30 feet. He put the shotgun back in the rack, placed the car into drive and pulled a slow U-turn. He and John locked eyes for a brief second, and Jimmy peeled away, never looking back.

John stood for a moment watching as his older brother Officer Jimmy Caul drove away. After a few seconds he hobbled across Kelsey Road and disappeared into the high corn, wondering how he was going to get to either his car or back to his home that was nearly three miles away.

CHAPTER
- 21 -

Dwayne found Amy completely by accident.

He ran to her as she stepped from an old car in the driveway of a two-story, tan-colored house. She was truly in shock to see him.

The Deer Park police, wanting to get the ex-con out of their elite community, had driven him to nearby Lake Zurich and dumped him and a $100 off at a Holiday Inn on Route 12. Officer Hynek was given orders to watch as Dwayne walked into the lobby and got himself a room for the night. Officer Hynek had done his job and driven away.

But Dwayne didn't get a room. When he stepped into the lobby, he only pretended to speak with the desk clerk before walking back outside. He kept the $100 for food money, walked around back of the Holiday Inn and set up a small encampment in a wooded area near a creek a few hundred yards away from the hotel.

He'd been living there for nearly a week now without any trouble. And in a bit of kismet, it was only a few blocks away from where Amy was residing with her friends. There seemed like a lot of kismet going on in Lake Zurich for some reason.

Dwayne had to fend for himself, so he foraged on a daily basis in the neighborhood around his campsite. People out here in Lake Zurich must have still felt confident that no one would mess with their stuff. That's why 25 percent of them left their garage doors open all day long.

He hadn't found a whole bunch to steal, other than a tent and a scoped pellet gun. If nothing else, he'd be out of the elements and able to hunt for a fat squirrel or two to supplement the $100 food money the cops had given him.

He was wandering the neighborhood, looking for more cash-producing stuff to steal, when he saw his sister drive past him. He had to sprint, cutting through some yards, but he eventually caught up to her.

After an awkward reunion, complete with mechanical hugs and kisses, they headed for the basement of Lori and Jerry's home to catch up.

"You can't stay here," she said for the third time.

"You hear what happened to old Deaton, that fucker?" he asked. "I shot his kneecap clean off - he had to quit being a cop. You'd think he'd be done for, right? Maybe collect a pension or some shit and hole up in a trailer, drinking until he stops breathing or something, right? Nope. That man wound up getting a desk job at a bank. Now he's the VP. Shit…I done him a favor, for goddamned sure."

"Dwayne, I have to leave soon. I'm job hunting-"

"No shit, me too! I figure if I can crash here for a night or two. That would set me up fine."

Amy finally took a good look at her brother and decided not to push any more for him to leave. She'd be able to explain the situation to Lori and Jerry, they'd understand and allow Dwayne to stay for a few nights.

"Are you hungry?" she asked. But it was a stupid question. Dwayne was skin and bones, the poor guy.

Dwayne didn't want to burden her with the gory details of his incarceration, release and sojourn to connect with his little sister. Some of those details included near daily gang fights in prison, and living off of raw field crops as he hitchhiked his way north to locate his kin.

He smiled and said, "Sure am, little sis!"

Amy felt a wave of familiar warmth as she took in the sight of her brother. She hadn't been around him in nearly 20 years, but it all came rushing back to her. Dwayne was a criminal, but he was probably one of the most positive people she had ever known. If he was emotionally down, it never lasted too long, or maybe he had conditioned himself to be an excellent actor.

Either way, it made her smile and take in a deep breath in an attempt to control the tears that were forming in her eyes.

"Have you ever had an Italian beef sandwich?" she asked.

CHAPTER
- 22 -

He snapped the Vicodin pill down the middle, tossed half into his mouth and washed it down with a chug of milk directly from the carton while standing at the open fridge.

The blood began trickling again from his left nostril, and he dabbed at it with a dish towel from the sink. He then dropped the other half of the pill back into the bottle.

Jimmy sat at the kitchen table of John's and his childhood home and sipped whiskey from a coffee cup. His police uniform shirt was unbuttoned, his hair a mess and the knuckles on his right hand were bloody.

John stepped away from the fridge and broken glass crunched under his shoes. He pushed the remnants of a shattered, wooden chair away from a slightly less damaged chair and took a seat.

The kitchen looked like a minor disaster area. Fifteen minutes prior, Jimmy had launched a punch at John's nose. John was shaky, but he held his ground the best he could, trading quick jabs with his brother. In their struggle, they had knocked several glass and porcelain knickknacks from the counters. Mostly roosters, but a few apples bit the dust, too.

Jimmy had flung John across the now mangled, wooden chair and gotten him into a headlock. That's when they settled and finally separated.

And now Jimmy leaned back and allowed his eyes to scan the sights of the kitchen and the décor which hadn't changed since the last time he was here, 20 years earlier. He shook his head as he took in the country roosters and apples fighting it out for his attention.

And the two brothers simply sat there - silently.

John hoped that the half-Vike would alleviate the shakes that were wracking his body. But he knew from experience that it would take about 30 minutes or so for the drug to take effect, if it were to work at all. It was a backslide in his attempt to discontinue taking the drug, but he had to rethink the process of stopping. Maybe stepping down gradually would be better for his physical and emotional states.

His mind shifted to worrying about getting his car back before the cops found it and possibly linked him to the robbery - to all of the robberies. He wasn't ready for that to happen because all of the money hadn't been raised as of yet.

He could call a cab but would have to wait for an hour or two for it to arrive, since cab service was spotty way out in Balmoral.

He wasn't worried that his brother Jimmy would arrest him, or turn him in or drop an anonymous dime on him, though. Jimmy had a lot to lose if it ever got out that his brother John Caul was the Baby Face Robber. First to go would be his promotion to lieutenant and then probably his job altogether.

"So this is all a big "fuck you" to the town, is that it?" said Jimmy. "Why not write a letter to the editor of the paper, or something? You have to do it this way? I don't get it."

"What would you know? You didn't do the inexcusable and have to live with it every day," said John. "They never let me forget," he added.

"Why not move out of town?"

"And go where, Jimmy? The house is all I have," he lied.

Jimmy didn't know about the "tidy sum" of money John had made through the stock market. John wasn't going to tell him about it now, not today, anyway - maybe not ever. Jimmy always thought that John had plowed through the life insurance money their dad left behind and that he had estranged himself from.

"I can't find a decent job because of the MS, you know that. I'd miss too many days whenever the vertigo sets in. I'd get fired time and time again. The town's got to pay for what they've done to me for all of these years. Don't worry, though, no one's going to get physically hurt."

Jimmy said, "Not in Balmoral, but what about the places where you've shoved a gun in people's faces? John, come on."

John ignored Jimmy's statement and said, "But I do intend on embarrassing the shit out of them so they'll know that I got the upper hand. Doing a few years in jail is nothing to me. I bet the embarrassment will never wear off for them, though. I hope it doesn't, anyway."

"What embarrassment? You're losing it."

"You know the way the people here in town think that they're better than the folks in the surrounding towns. You know firsthand. You work here but live in Crystal Lake. You hear the way people talk about all the other suburbs in the area. How they lack charm. How the houses are ugly and cheaply built. You hear this stuff, and you know it."

"Shit, John."

"The news media will eat this up. They'll cover the crap out of this story once I blow the lid off of it. They'll make total asses out of Balmoral folks. People love seeing upper class people fail."

"What, are we talking about a handful of people who like to give you shit? What?"

"No, Jimmy, it's more than a handful."

Jimmy was just about to call "bullshit" on his younger brother, but he pulled up short. He knew exactly what John was talking about in regards to how people had treated him over the years.

Any person living a daily life in town would know it, too. John was a pariah. Up until this moment Jimmy had never really put a lot of thought into what his brother was going through. Jimmy sipped more whiskey, studied his younger brother's face and said, "What are we going to do, brother?"

John leaned toward the sink and picked up the dish towel to dab at the trickling blood again and said, "I told you. I'm going to save the Fourth of July celebration. I want the townspeople to have a great time. I want them to feel self-satisfied and important for what they've accomplished yet again. And after it's over, I'm going public with what I did. I'll admit to every last detail. It'll deflate the air out of their lives for damned sure. I want them to feel the embarrassment and shame the way I do every day. I've had it!"

"You'll do some serious time. Probably five or more years, easy."

"I don't care. That's the point," said John.

"I heard a rumor about someone dropping off cash, but no one's officially talking about it at the village, you know," said Jimmy.

That struck a nerve with John who had heard Lou at Dink's talking about the money. But even Lou said that it was all talk so far.

Jimmy added, "I heard that asshole councilman, Keith Michaels, may have some involvement, but they're all pretty tight-lipped over there at the municipal building. No one can find any extra money on the books. It's probably all bullshit."

"You think someone's keeping it for themselves? A village official?" John wondered aloud with his demeanor changing from semi-confident to confused to downright fearful. "Which one is Keith Michaels?" asked John.

"He's the one that looks like a human weasel," said Jimmy.

In that instant, while John was at a low point, Jimmy knew he could get away with it.

He could easily kill his brother right here in the kitchen and dispose of the body in the woods of southern Wisconsin where no one would ever find it. He'd stop the Baby Face Robber and save his job promotion and his new, hefty pay raise in one fell swoop. He could accomplish all of this for the cost of a 50-cent bullet and a gallon or two of gasoline.

His girls could quit the part-time jobs they'd taken in Evanston to help defray some of the school costs they had incurred. The Fourth of July celebration may not take place, but he could live with that. It was a pain in the ass to work anyway, with all the drunken, firework-tossing assholes he had to deal with year in and year out.

However a sea change occurred in Jimmy's mind as he continued to observe his brother. John's world seemed to be crumbling around him. Jimmy watched as his little brother absently worked his jaw muscles – this little brother he never really stood up for when they were kids.

Jimmy's mind raced back to the old days back in this house on Coleridge, with their cold mother and her fake concern for her children, and their emotionally absent father and his inane joking.

Jimmy had gotten out of the house as soon as the Marines would have him, but John didn't leave. Why?

Maybe John was stronger than Jimmy could ever be or give him credit for. John stayed after Mary died, to watch after their father. He could've left when he was 18 and ventured off on his own. John didn't have to stick around and see Bernie, who, after Mary's death, was a mere shell of himself, waste away for the next ten years leading up to his death. Jimmy couldn't keep from wondering what that grown-up, real world pressure could do to a young mind. But all he could say at the moment was-

"Come on, I'll get you back to your car."

CHAPTER
- 23 -

Jimmy used the Balmoral police car to drop John off where he had left the Chevy wagon.

By that time John had showered and changed clothes, and Jimmy had drunk nearly a pot of coffee to combat the effects of the whiskey he downed in John's kitchen after their altercation.

They had come to an uneasy agreement that Jimmy wouldn't turn John in if John promised not to rob any more businesses for the time being. Each side of the equation had a lot to lose; John, his chance to fuck over the town he'd grown to hate, and Jimmy, his promotion to lieutenant and all that that would bring with it.

They decided to reconvene in a few days to try and figure out what to ultimately do to help both of their causes. The brothers needed time to lick their wounds and do some soul searching. In the car they didn't talk much, other than John giving Jimmy directions on how to get to where he stashed his car.

Oddly enough, Jimmy was sort of proud of his little brother for how he had confounded the cops to this point. He knew that John was a brilliant person, and how, when they were kids, that brilliance was threatening to him. But now, he actually felt a strange, brotherly affection for John in a "this son of a bitch is good at what he does" way.

***

John, alone in the Chevy wagon, drove eastbound on Route 22 and entered the town limits of Lake Zurich. He wasn't quite right in the head. The half a Vike helped curb some of the withdrawal symptoms but only to a minor degree. Once or twice during his drive, he forgot where he was going and what he was going to do.

That was it - there was a Wal-Mart in Lake Zurich where he could pick up another cheap windbreaker. And there was a gun shop nearby that always had excellent deals on cheap 9mm pistols. He'd have to wait out the Brady rule but that was okay, because he was not going to break the agreement that he and his older brother, Jimmy, had made. There would be no more robberies until they got back together.

Luckily, the last gun he had used he had procured through the Vike vine and the serial numbers were filed off, so it couldn't be traced back to him. If he did decide to go the legal route in purchasing his next gun, that wouldn't be the case, though.

Turning north on Route 12, he wondered if a handheld, electric, drum-filing tool would do the job in erasing the serial numbers. He wasn't quite ready to turn himself in or get caught for pulling off the robberies and needed every advantage at his disposal to make sure everything went as planned.

As he drove he looked toward the parking lot where the grocery store and Italian beef place stood. It didn't instantly register who the beautiful woman was as she got out of the ten-year-old car in the parking lot. She was with a sallow and scrawny-looking man in his forties who appeared as if he'd just been saved from a mine shaft in some South American country.

***

Amy ordered for herself and Dwayne.

They sat at a table by the window of the Italian beef place. It was a kitschy little eatery created from the shell of a former ten-minute oil change garage. They were enjoying delicious Italian beef sandwiches and crispy waffle fries.

"Not a one of 'em wants to leave, you know," said Dwayne.

Amy was uncomfortable talking about family because she felt, from time to time, that she abandoned them although she really hadn't.

Dwayne added, "They never even left for a little while to at least explore. 'Course, when I left, it wasn't by choice." He smiled sheepishly. "But I'm here now, ain't I?"

Amy and Dwayne got caught up on family and old, small-town friends and what they were all doing nowadays. They soon discovered that nearly 20 years of absence had done nothing to change things back in Jackson. But both agreed that that was how it should be. The beauty of Jackson was that it didn't really change – not ever.

"No one could blame you for leaving, sis. You did the right thing," Dwayne said as he took a juicy bite of sandwich.

She nearly choked on a sweet pepper when she saw him yank the front door open and step inside.

He looked like he hadn't slept in a few nights. The deep circles under his eyes were quite prominent. But she quickly admitted something to herself, though - he was a good-looking man that she had a hard time taking her eyes off of. And now he was angling right toward her table. She chewed and swallowed the food in her mouth as quickly as she could.

"Hi, can we talk?" he said.

Dwayne didn't like the way the guy crowded their table.

"Wanna back it up, my man?"

In the State Pen, Dwayne would've put John on his ass and asked him later what he wanted after the dust had settled. But he knew things were more civilized out in the world, so he controlled his aggression for now. He turned and noticed the expression on his sister's face. She liked this dude. Well, shit, this was an altogether, different situation.

"I've got to, ah, use the can. Be right back," he said as he excused himself.

Dwayne got up and left. Amy finally nodded to the empty seat next to her. John sat down and measured his words very carefully.

"I'm a Vicodin addict."

"No shit…"

"But you have to know why."

"Why should I care?"

"Please hear me out for just 30 seconds."

"You've got until my brother comes back," she said.

"Oh, that's your brother. I thought…right, um, you see… well, how do I put this?"

"Better start talking," Amy said.

"I have multiple sclerosis," he said for the first time to anyone other than his brother, Jimmy. "Unfortunately for me, I'm in constant pain," he added.

She believed him.

Who couldn't? Especially after he told her all about how the disease had taken so much away from him. He explained about how the doctors, trying to help his liver function, limited the amount of pain medication they would prescribe in hopes of not creating a new problem in addition to the MS.

He told her how he had disregarded their attempts at curbing his Vicodin intake, and how he went in search of illegal sources of the drug to alleviate his relentless pain. But the bottom line always circled back to the fact that he was an addict. He admitted that to someone other than the mirror for the first time. It felt like a solid, first step toward normalcy.

Amy knew that he wasn't acting or putting on some sort of ruse. John was sincere. But she still wasn't sure she wanted to be involved with him.

"I'm Dwayne, Amy's brother."

John stood said, "John," and shook hands with Dwayne and they both sat.

"What are you going to do now, John?" she said.

But John didn't want to talk any more about his problem, especially with Dwayne at the table. Amy understood and quickly changed the subject.

"So my brother, Dwayne, here is looking for work. Do you know of anyone who may be hiring?" asked Amy.

John nodded "thanks" to Amy for not pressing any more, and he turned to Dwayne and said, "What line of work are you in, Dwayne?"

Dwayne smiled a big, toothy grin and said, "The paying kind."

***

"I'd like to ask you to dinner," John said as he and Amy stood next to her car in the parking lot.

Dwayne, across the lot, had made an instant friend with a 30-year-old man who had pulled up to the Italian beef place in a brand-new BMW. The man was more than happy to show Dwayne all the cool features of the car. Dwayne was completely in awe of the technology. He had seen car commercials in the State Pen while watching sports on TV but inspecting the cars up close was much better.

"So ask," she said.

"Is tonight good for you?"

As she nodded, a thought came to him. "How did it go at the car dealership?"

"That didn't work out. I'm still on the search. I'd take anything right now. But I'd really like something in management or with the chance of getting into management," she said.

"I remember your saying that at the bar. I know things are tough right now," he said, before stopping abruptly. John was looking directly at a Franklin Finch Ice Cream/Dip Doughnuts franchise that was situated across Route 12 from the parking lot where they stood.

In his travels around the northwest suburbs of Chicago, he'd seen several of these buildings – small, boxy affairs with colorful signage. And just as quickly, a second and third thought came to him. John, in his part-time but very lucrative job as a stock market player, had read where these types of franchises could be cash cows. They were fairly easy to get off the ground, and the training needed to own and run the franchise was provided by the parent company for a start-up fee, of course.

The third thought was that he remembered seeing a segment on TV about a franchise trade show that was coming to the McCormick Place Convention Center in Chicago. John had experienced another kismet-like moment in Lake Zurich.

A fourth idea suddenly dawned on him. But before he could fully complete the thought, Amy gently grasped John's elbow bringing him back to the conversation.

"Let's meet at the Irish bar in Balmoral at eight," she said.

The thoughts bombarding John's mind made him smile. He hadn't felt quite this positive about doing anything since first conjuring up the "robbery to help save the Fourth of July celebration" idea and meeting Amy. But what made the thoughts pinging around in his brain more satisfying this time was that it was all legal. Okay, mostly legal.

"But we'll eat somewhere else, is that okay?"

"See you at eight," she said.

CHAPTER
- 24 -

Like most who excelled in that particular space, Brick was a no-nonsense kind of drug dealer.

He had met the dentist through a mutual friend, a person who had turned Brick onto the Vike vine. Brick learned that the dentist had been run out of business in Lake Zurich by some dude wearing a baby face mask, and now he was ready to start up another operation.

He needed an equity partner, though. The dentist would provide the legal, medical front and actual distribution arm, handing out the merchandise and collecting the money from customers. The equity partner, Brick, would provide the capital and drugs needed to get the operation outfitted.

Brick was an only child. His father, a retired Chicago police officer, and his mother, now deceased, was a homemaker. He grew up in the Pill Hill neighborhood on the South Side of Chicago. It was once an affluent, urban oasis occupied by doctors who serviced the neighborhood hospital, thus the name, Pill Hill.

Unfortunately, like so many other city neighborhoods, it slowly changed over the years. After the doctors began looking elsewhere for housing, the area stagnated. It's still solidly middle-class, but not nearly the same as it was in its heyday.

Being an only child, Brick was spoiled rotten. He didn't have the hardscrabble upbringing nearly his entire drug-dealing underlings had experienced. And he didn't get started in the drug trade to rebel against his police officer father, either. He simply didn't want to put in the hours his father did to make a living.

A 12-year-old Brick couldn't keep his eyes off of the fat cat dealers and pimps who traveled through his area. Driving their Caddies and surrounded by sweet bitches. Brick knew there was an easier way to success than punching a clock every day.

When he was 15, he started his first weed-slinging operation with a $500 investment from his own bank account. Brick took the initial $500 and parlayed that into nearly $12,000 in a matter of a few weeks' time. He never looked back.

There was a price to pay for his new, lucrative, business operation. His mother, a heart patient, began experiencing a rapid succession of setbacks soon after Brick took a .22 round to his head. The bullet ricocheted off his skull and did very little damage, but the stressful nature of the event, while providing Brick with his nickname, "head as hard as a brick," did eventually kill off his mother.

Brick arranged for the person responsible for delivering the .22 round to his skull a more instantaneous form of death the day after his mother passed.

By 17, Brick was making nearly $250,000 a year. His father loved him, but he couldn't stand having a drug dealer living under his roof.

So Brick set up shop on the West Side of Chicago and flourished, branching out into the western and northwestern suburbs. And as a testament to his business acumen, Brick never identified himself with the myriad street gangs in the Chicago area. He was an anomaly among his drug-dealing brethren - an independent businessman.

He accomplished this independence by not undercutting the

prices of other gang-affiliated dealers and only operating in areas they didn't. His territories were spread out from Wauconda to Downers Grove to the West Side of Chicago, but that was okay. It provided him with the peace of mind in knowing that no one was gunning for him.

Now Brick waited next to his Escalade on the western edge of the Woodfield Mall's massive parking lot and considered his surroundings.

He tried to imagine what the area had looked like in 1956 when Schaumburg was founded. How the original 100 or so residents lived day to day in what the late, great Chicago Tribune writer Mike Royko deemed, "The land beyond O'Hare."

Brick figured it was mostly cornfields and apple orchards way back when, but now he gazed upon nearly three million square feet of retail space under one roof. The mall itself was surrounded by an ocean of satellite stores, mini-malls and paved parking lots.

"Place is fucking ugly, man," he said as his business associate, Aaron, a tall man with a 1000-yard stare, walked in his direction. "Junior and Peaches better keep their fucking eyes open, my man, else…well, you don't wanna know the what else."

"Junior fucks it up, he's gone. No problem with me," said Aaron as he scanned the parking lot for the Chevy wagon they were awaiting. "Nothin's whack. We're cool."

"Was Peaches always a fuck up? I mean when you were kids?"

"Don't sweat it, Brick. My little bro messes up - I said I'll take care of it."

Brick's mind drifted again. This guy named John had used the same Vike vine to send out a coded message looking for buyers of large quantities of Vikes. Through another series of messages, each relaying a cell phone number hidden one digit at a time in the body of the text, Brick had connected by phone and set up this meeting. The John dude said he wanted to unload a mess of Vicodin. He had thousands of pills on hand.

Brick's objective in this transaction was a bit different than what the guy in the powder blue station wagon's would be, he was sure of that.

Brick was going to hold onto his cash, kill the deliverer of the Vikes and drive away with the goods. So what if it took a bit more gas money to get way the fuck out here in Schaumburg. It would be worth it.

CHAPTER

- 25 -

As John drove the old station wagon east on Coleridge, he couldn't help but happily daydream about how he would acquire some solid employment for Amy and possibly provide her a future in management.

He was going to meet this man named Brick at Woodfield Mall and sell him all of the Vicodin he had stolen from the dentist in Lake Zurich. From his years of misuse, John was quite adept at pricing illegal Vicodin, estimating that he had in his possession nearly $75,000 worth of the drug. That would be enough to get him solidly on the path to launch a Franklin Finch Ice Cream/Dip Doughnuts franchise.

He'd seen a segment on WGN about the lucrative, fast-food franchise a few days before meeting Amy. And just that morning he'd done another Google search on the franchise trade show coming to McCormick Place, scoping out the map where the Franklin Finch Ice Cream/Dip Doughnuts booth would be set up. He didn't want to waste any time when he got to the enormous convention center. He wanted to take Amy directly to the booth and talk turkey with the company representatives on how they could get started.

Slowing for the stop sign at Coleridge and Balmoral, John saw a white flash as an SUV careened north, doing 50 in a 25. In that brief moment he caught a glimpse of the driver. Danny.

The Land Rover took a harrowing and tilting right on Trussell Street.

Instead of turning south and heading toward Woodfield Mall, John took a quick left on Balmoral and a right on Trussell. He slowed the station wagon as he neared Cook Street, looking north and south. Peering south on Cook, John noticed the brake lights of the Land Rover flash as it pulled into a driveway halfway down the block.

He parked a few houses away and took in the sight of the beautiful home Danny had just walked into. Inexplicably, John was angry. The kid was obviously not destitute, as his choice of clothing would suggest. The home, a 100-year-old frame house that was impeccably rehabbed, was easily worth over a million dollars.

***

Danny slowly closed the front door and listened for any activity in what should be an empty house.

All was clear.

He put the keys to the Land Rover carefully back on the hook near the front door, making sure they were in the exact same position as they were before he had stolen them.

His mother, Sharon, was a stickler for details. Having the Land Rover insignia facing right instead of left, as she had placed the keys the night before, would be enough for her to know they had been tampered with.

He kicked his dirty shoes off right there at the front door and began to head for the kitchen, when the front doorbell chimed. Circling back, Danny tried to look out the front window to see who was at the door but only made out a shoulder of the man standing there.

As soon as he cracked the door open, John shoved his way

into the house and slammed the door shut in back of him.

"What the fuck, man?"

"I was thinking the same thing," said John.

"Get out!"

"Why were you following me? You think your parents would be interested in knowing you were out joyriding? Do you even have a driver's license?"

"I'm not going to tell anyone what you did," said Danny.

John took in the sight of the terrified teen and said, "I'm doing this all for a good reason, okay. You have to know that. I'm going to save the Fourth of July celebration."

"I thought you were cool, man. I thought…"

They both jumped when the back door opened, and Danny's mother walked into the house. She didn't notice John at first because of where he stood just around the doorframe from Danny.

"Hi, sweetie. The train was so crowded. I almost didn't get a seat. Did you get something to eat? There's leftover lasagna from last night in the fridge. I need to head over and pick up your baby brother at preschool." She stepped closer to give Danny a peck on the cheek when she noticed John. "Oh! Hello."

"Hi, I'm John Caul. How are you?"

They shook hands but Sharon wasn't sure about the situation. There was palpable tension brewing between her son and John, but Sharon chose not to pry at this time. She had actually seen John on a few occasions around town and thought he was quite handsome – sexy, even.

She noticed John the most often when he shopped at the Gemstone and always wondered why the cashiers would hurriedly shut their lanes down when they saw John approaching with his shopping cart. He seemed like a very cordial and smiley sort. The sour expressions the cashiers and other employees at the food store exhibited toward John never made sense to her.

And who was she kidding, since her husband Donald had transferred to this area with his job, he had little time for Sharon. She was being ignored not only through a lack of conversation in the home but in the marital bed as well. John was handsome, that was certain to Sharon. But of late, she had noticed that there were a lot of handsome men in Balmoral.

John finally said, "Your son volunteered to help me maintain the little league ball fields, and we were discussing the hours. I hope I didn't startle you."

Sharon became pleasantly surprised. John's interest in helping her son Danny made this Balmoral man even more appealing. She said, "Danny? You never told me about this. So, mister…?"

"John Caul. John." He turned and looked Danny directly in the eye and continued, "Danny's been a lot of help. I can really count on him."

Danny was truly terrified and about to spill the beans about John's history to his mom. As he opened his mouth to blurt out the details of the Baby Face Robber's fucked-up robbery attempt, John quickly continued, "When Danny gets his driver's license, he'll be even more help because he can legally drive the mower around town as needed."

"Oh, but that's a year away," said Sharon.

John and Danny's eyes met and locked, and John said, "Huh. A whole year. Really? How about that…Danny?"

CHAPTER
- 26 -

"I used to be on the job in Evanston," he said to Jimmy the cop.

"I retired a few years back." Retired, fired and almost put in jail, whatever, this tough-looking, Balmoral copper was buying it, thought Enright. "Now I do my own thing."

Jimmy, sitting at the small, U-shaped counter of Dink's Diner, had a bad feeling about the guy sitting across from him. There was something wrong with the guy. The cashier at the Gemstone on Main thought the same. That's why she had called Jimmy on his cell phone after this Enright character stood at her register while buying a single pack of gum and asked her all sorts of probing questions about life in Balmoral. The cashier thought that maybe the guy was a burglar casing the town or something.

Jimmy sensed it, too. There was something crooked about him. It was more than the way he dressed, wearing an ill-fitting and cheap sport coat and off-brand blue jeans. It was the way he never looked a person directly in the eyes. Enright always looked a few degrees to the right or left of the person he was addressing. It placed Jimmy on guard.

"These Baby Face robberies are something, huh?" said Enright, noticing the way the freshly-sipped coffee caught in Jimmy's throat. "You okay?"

Jimmy took a sip of water and cleared his throat, "Fine, thanks."

Enright made sure that no one else was listening as he leaned forward for some low volume "cop talk."

"I hear the guy mostly likes robbing breakfast restaurants... like this one. But he's hitting everything around this town right here. Just never in this town itself. Strange, huh? I'm sure they have a task force set up to catch the fucker, though, right? I mean, I've been out of the game for so long, but I figured that was the cop's first move."

When Jimmy didn't offer up an answer, because there was no Baby Face Robber task force in place, Enright knew that his source in the Buffalo Grove police department was right. He was the only Baby Face Robber hunter at this point. He smiled and waved a "no need to answer" Jimmy's way.

Jimmy quickly finished off his coffee, stood, put a couple of dollars next to his plate, nodded a goodbye to Enright and made his way to the cash register.

Lou met him at the front counter. Jimmy handed a twenty to Lou to pay for his tab. And as Lou made change, he said, "You get tired of Curious George over there, too? He asks a lot of questions."

Jimmy said, "Yeah? What do you think he's up to?"

"He asks me what's different around here."

"What do you mean?"

"Like, is there something new happening in town. Is something wrong here, stuff like that. Weird shit. And he asks forceful, too. I don't like that. This is my place. He's police or something?"

"I don't think so," said Jimmy.

"We know the only thing different is that we won't have the Fourth of July celebration in summer. But why would anyone else care about that, huh?"

Jimmy pulled away from Dink's Diner in his police car in time to see John, driving the old Chevy wagon, turn on Coleridge, followed closely by a black Escalade, and soon another, and a few seconds later, yet another black Escalade.

His first inclination was to keep driving south on Balmoral and not to let the sight of the three SUVs following his brother get to him, odd as it was.

In the past, he'd not even look twice at something out of place with his younger brother, but things were different for Jimmy now. He was interested in what John was up to. Jimmy had self-preservation on his mind.

***

Dwayne, in Amy's 10-year-old car, spotted John's station wagon turning onto a street up ahead. He smiled to himself, thinking, "What the hell, maybe I can catch up to him and shoot the shit for a few minutes before applying for the next job."

Dwayne's employment search wasn't yielding too many results up to this point even though he'd only spent a few hours at it. There were fast-food job openings here and there, but those franchises usually frowned upon hiring convicted felons. He knew his best bet would be getting a gig at some mom-and-pop place in a town like Balmoral.

He thought the area was beautiful. Not Kentucky, rolling hills beautiful, but quite appealing all the same. He'd never been to any New England small towns, but he had seen photos and movies filmed there and thought Balmoral was pretty damned close to that kind of quintessential, small-town splendor.

There was a slow-moving, Balmoral cop car in front of him so he played it cool, holding back from his first impulse to pass him. That's when he noticed John's old Chevy wagon turn on a street up ahead followed by three, black SUVs.

The Balmoral cop car turned onto the same street. Dwayne, trying to avoid any unwanted attention by the police, drove to the next street and took that to Dundee Avenue circling back to

Coleridge. He arrived on Coleridge in time to see three, black Escalades park in front of a house with either a bad paint job or some sort of stains all over it.

It was obvious to Dwayne that the SUVs were following the Chevy wagon. Before long the cop car drove slowly past with the cop himself looking down the house's shitty-looking driveway. Dwayne played it cool as the cop drove past, tossing a wave and a grin.

***

The garage door was wide open and Brick had a .40-caliber Glock semi-automatic pistol pushed into John's neck.

Aaron, and his two other cohorts, Peaches, a short muscular dude, and Junior, a rangy and dangerous-appearing man, ripped up the inside of John's garage.

Peaches picked up one of John's junk-based metal sculptures and admired it.

"Dude!" said Brick, and Peaches put the sculpture down and continued to search.

"Just tell us, man," Brick said to John. "We don't need the hassle. Where's the shit?" He pressed the gun harder into John's neck and added, "You don't, either. We take it and go. Easy as that."

John nodded to the metal cabinet near the weed whacker hanging by a hook on the wall. Aaron stepped over to open the door and extracted a small single bottle of Vicodin. "What the fuck? This is it?" he said.

John, for some odd reason, wasn't afraid.

He knew these drug dealers wanted the drugs and not him dead until they actually had their mitts on the goods. So he was confident that he was in a good spot, being that the bulk of the Vikes were now hidden in the little league field's equipment shack where no one would look for them.

But Brick pushed John into the wall of the garage and pointed the Glock at his chest, and said, "That's your large quantity, one fucking bottle? We wasted good gas money for this shit?"

126

Okay, now John was scared; he figured it all wrong. "Well, hell," he thought, "they are going to kill me." He didn't see his life pass in front of his eyes or anything, but an urge to urinate grew and grew to an uncomfortable level.

***

Jimmy sat in his idling police car at the corner of Dundee and Coleridge wondering if he should go and see if John was okay. His guard was definitely up, especially after interacting with that asshole Enright back at Dink's Diner. The three SUVs now parked in front of John's house were the toppers, though.

He couldn't let go of the nagging feeling that his brother was in danger. He pushed the thought aside and wondered what would happen if people found out that his brother was the Baby Face Robber and how that would screw him out of his upcoming job promotion.

What the hell was he doing allowing these negative thoughts to seep into his mind? And, hell, this was Balmoral in the middle of a warm and sunny day. What could be wrong? He shook the thoughts away and drove off.

***

"Hey, guys," was all he said, enough for John to immediately recognize the Kentucky drawl and the owner of the voice.

Peaches, Aaron and Junior all extracted their own guns and pointed them toward the voice but none of them could see anything. That is until the barrel of the long rifle poked from around the corner of John's house opposite of the driveway.

"Eh, eh, drop 'em," said Dwayne.

And when they didn't, Dwayne turned toward the neighbor's house and said, "Ernie! Roger! You got a bead, guys?"

That's when all the combatants in the garage turned to see the glint of sunshine off a scope and two more rifle barrels aimed right at them from the dense bushes of the neighbor's house. The combatant's confusion was nearly comical, their heads swiveled, their guns pointed here and there.

"Fella's, just take what you got and go. No need to make this shitty," said Dwayne, the lackadaisical confidence in his voice enough to punch his point home.

Peaches leaned over and began placing his gun on the ground and Aaron, the bottle of Vikes on top of the Chevy wagon.

"Keep it. We don't need your guns or shit. We got plenty of our own. Remember that," said Dwayne.

Peaches straightened, and he, Brick and the others put their guns away and quickly made their way down the driveway toward their SUVs.

**

Jimmy felt another layer of relief when he saw the four, tough-looking men saunter to their SUVs.

The largest of the four, a man with a scar along his forehead, turned before he got behind the wheel of an SUV and made a gun with his hand, pretend fired and smiled.

John, who stood close to his house, waved in a nonchalant, "toodle-loo" fashion.

The bad thoughts had crept back into the forefront of his mind as he drove away a few minutes earlier. Now Jimmy wasn't in his cop car. He had parked it on Monument Street and walked the half block to the hiding place he'd chosen on the porch of a house five down from John's home.

Continuing to peer through binoculars, Jimmy waited for John to go back inside his house before making his way to his police car and continuing his normally scheduled day.

**

At John's kitchen table, Dwayne untwisted picture-hanging wire off of the downside end of a shepherd's hook and released the pellet gun scope into his hand.

It was a good thing that some folks in Balmoral were like the ones in Lake Zurich – leaving their garages open all day long. And that this neighbor in particular, the one whose garage Dwayne had foraged through, was a gardening enthusiast.

Upon seeing the dire straits that John was in, Dwayne had improvised his way into creating an army of three out of one scoped pellet gun, some wire and the neighbors' penchant for having way too many shepherd's hooks in their yard. The pellet gun lay across the kitchen table and now Dwayne placed the shepherd's hook alongside it.

A shaky John stood at the sink and started taking a whole tablet of Vicodin, thought better and snapped it in half. He downed the half pill with a chug of cold milk from the carton.

"How long have you been hooked?" asked Dwayne.

John took a seat at the table in the now cleaned and repaired kitchen and said, "Who knows?"

He noticed the grim expression his new friend was displaying and added, "A couple of years. I just admitted it to myself is what I really meant to say."

Dwayne started putting the scope back on the pellet gun and said, "You going to meetings or talking to anyone about it?"

"I'm talking to you, aren't I?" John said with a twinge of frustration and anger. After seeing the hurt in Dwayne's eyes, he added, "Sorry."

Dwayne waved it off. If this was a year ago and he was in the Kentucky State Penitentiary, John's ass would've been on the floor about now. But today, in John's kitchen, Dwayne was a softer and more forgiving man.

It was also that he liked John right from the start, especially after he made his play back at the Italian beef place. In the past, if a dude had walked up behind Dwayne like John had, he'd have to deal with the certain swift pain he'd receive. But Dwayne felt an odd sort of kinship with John because the man was looking out for his sister, Amy. And to Dwayne, that made all the difference in the world. In his mind, he and John were instant friends, brothers, really.

Dwayne asked, "You got two or three bedrooms here?"

CHAPTER
- 27 -

Sitting in the oaken den of their million dollar home and sipping Earl Grey tea, Danny's parents, Donald and Sharon, were perplexed and beginning to overanalyze the situation. But that was their nature especially when they were feeling a lack of control in their lives.

Danny had not left his room in the past few days, except for bathroom breaks. They had to bring his meals to him. He wouldn't discuss what was bothering him. And he didn't even want to play with his younger brother, something he loved doing more than anything else.

Danny's emotional freeze-out started after that man named John Caul had stopped by their home to speak with him about volunteering. Sharon could see that her son was off his game, stammering and not his usual and confident self.

Donald, measuring his words carefully, said, "Do you think there was abuse?"

Sharon didn't want to even consider it.

She knew that this situation didn't fit the pattern of stranger abuse, for the perpetrator to actually step foot in the home of the one they abuse. It was completely out of character. That type of behavior was usually observed in family and close friend abuse.

Honestly, she thought, John Caul was a perfectly normal man - handsome, polite and self-assured. She had dealt with abusers in her years as a therapist and John just didn't fit the mold. But of course, she could be dead wrong.

"Maybe we should call the police," she said.

***

Danny was acting like a confused, little kitten. The idea of not being in control of his situation as it related to that older dude, John, totally knocked him off his usual, smartass game.

That fucker was the Baby Face Robber he had heard about on the news. But Danny thought he seemed so cool, how could he be pulling off armed robberies? Danny's 15-year-old brain just couldn't put all the pieces together. The guy lived in Balmoral - weren't people around here well-off? Why would he need to steal from others? He volunteered all the time, cutting grass and shit. What the fuck?

He wondered if he should tell his parents what he knew. But could that put his family in danger? He knew that when his little brother, Joseph, was born, he began acting out, but he loved that little guy now and didn't want to even think that anything bad could happen to him. He had to keep quiet and stay in the house for now. It was the only way to assure his family's safety.

But something deep within the reptilian recesses of his brain was churning. The thoughts confused and frightened him even more. And yet, he couldn't help wondering what it would be like to rob someone at gunpoint. He wondered what the adrenaline rush would feel like. He had placed himself in dangerous situations in the past, when making up stories about kids bigger, stronger and one hell of a lot meaner than he was, but the idea of gunplay fascinated him.

CHAPTER
- 28 -

Their dinner together was pleasant enough. They had met at the Irish pub in Balmoral, but John had chosen a French bistro in the quaint town of Long Grove for dinner. The bistro's specialty was coq au vin.

He did something he hadn't done since his father's funeral. He wore a sport coat.

Except for the ride over in the crappy old station wagon, Amy was impressed with the evening that John had planned. Amy, aware now of John's Vicodin taking ways, insisted on driving the old car herself to ensure they'd get around undamaged. He was a gentleman and she appreciated that, but she still needed to feel safe.

She was especially grateful that he had taken in her brother, Dwayne, and set him up in his second bedroom. And even after all the good that John had done, Amy couldn't help but think that John was not her type. He was handsome and, yes, sexy, but she usually went for the brasher men like her ex-husband, not the kindhearted and thoughtful ones. But John was growing on her.

In her quest for self-improvement, she had just finished

reading the Dr. Spencer Johnson book, "Who Moved My Cheese," and didn't want to fall into the "hem" way of thinking. She wanted to be a "haw," and she was most definitely on her way to getting there.

But now, a few days after their dinner date, as they made their way through the massive McCormick Place, all they could both think about was locating the Franklin Finch Ice Cream/Dip Doughnuts franchise booth.

The sea of booths laid out among the nearly three million square feet of exhibition space in front of them was daunting, and John was mentally kicking himself in the ass for not grabbing up one of the floor maps he was offered when they arrived.

The franchise show was in full bloom. Even in a down economy, people were interested in what they could invest in next. The ocean of people in attendance gave both John and Amy hope that something better was just around the corner.

John didn't really care what sort of place he was going to invest the Vicodin cash into. That is, once he found a proper buyer for the drugs. He was merely interested in getting Amy firmly on her way toward her dream of managing a business. So the decision to walk away from the Franklin Finch Ice Cream/Dip Doughnuts booth after a bland and no frills presentation was an easy one to make.

John could tell that Amy's heart wasn't really in the donut and ice cream venture anyway, and that was okay. That was his idea, not hers. He wanted to make sure that she was excited about her new job.

Nearly the entire time the boring man at the Franklin Finch Ice Cream/Dip Doughnuts booth was speaking, Amy had her eyes on the booth across the way. It was a color-filled and playful booth for The Kid Crew which was a franchise of sports-related, child care facilities.

At least that's what John was hoping she was looking at. The proprietor of the booth, a tall and handsome man, may have caught her eye, too.

John said, "And here I thought donuts and ice cream would be more stimulating." She laughed and John noticed her attention was fully on the Kid Crew booth.

"What's this?" he asked.

As John and Amy stepped over to The Kid Crew display, Amy could see that the tall, handsome man was the only person working the booth. He was busily working on his laptop and not really paying attention to anything around him.

As John and Amy moved closer, they could see that the man was typing away on a Facebook page, writing a comment under the photo of a 12-year-old girl who was sporting a playful smile. When he finally noticed Amy and John, he slapped the laptop closed.

"Hi. Um, welcome to The Kid Crew. I'm Henry. If you have any questions, please don't hesitate to ask. We have a comprehensive catalogue here, and some testimonial materials as well," he said.

Henry was a little nervous as he took in the sight of the beautiful Amy. But now Amy wasn't so sure about Henry. There was something off about the guy. He was handsome in a rugged, broad-shouldered sense, but Amy thought he was hiding something. This feeling was reinforced when Henry took the laptop and placed it under a table and out of view.

"Facebook, huh?" she said, nodding to the laptop. "I haven't gotten into that. You never really know who you may be talking to."

John was a bit confused by the angry change in Amy's demeanor, from excitement to near contempt for this Henry guy standing no more than three feet from her.

Henry could sense her anger as well, and his nervousness soon turned to a low-level anger of his own. "I was talking with my daughter."

Amy didn't believe him but didn't leave either. She wanted to know more about The Kid Crew and how the business worked.

She said, "Okay, Henry. Pitch us. What's your company all

about?"

And that's when Henry went on to make Amy feel like a squashed bug on a windshield for even hinting that Henry was up to nefarious, Facebook trolling.

The Kid Crew was Henry's wife's idea. A former corporate climber, Henry's wife, Liz, decided to start the very first Kid Crew center in her North Side Chicago neighborhood when their daughter, Emmy, was born 12 years ago. Liz quit her six-figure job and worked the same long hours attempting to launch Kid Crew. But the difference this time was that she was constantly with her infant daughter.

Tragically, Liz was killed two years later in an auto accident while the family was vacationing in Tucson. Henry was seriously injured, but Emmy was spared any real physical harm.

Due to his extensive permanent injuries, Henry wasn't able to keep his job as a trainer for the Northwestern University athletics department. He was, however, in good enough shape to keep The Kid Crew going and growing. Henry was not only an excellent trainer, he was seemingly a very savvy businessman, as well. He designed the franchise start-ups for The Kid Crew to be cost-effective and profitable, with a low, up front, cash outlay.

All Amy could do after Henry finished his pitch was point to the laptop and say, "Emmy?"

Henry smiled and nodded.

John, not wanting the "Kumbaya" moment to pass, wrote Henry a check for $35,000 on the spot. He was the proud owner of the new, Balmoral area Kid Crew franchise, with Amy as his soon-to-be general manager. The proceeds to cover the check came from John's investment account. He would replenish the $35,000 from the funds he'd get from selling the Vikes - piece of cake.

As John wrote the amount into his checkbook register, Henry passed Amy his card and said, "I wrote my cell phone number on the back in case you have questions after business hours." Before Amy could take the card, John unconsciously grabbed it and said,

"Thanks. We'll talk next week."

CHAPTER
- 29 -

After only a few days of having Dwayne as his roomie, John knew it was a mistake inviting him to stay. It wasn't that Dwayne was an ungracious houseguest. Quite the opposite was true. He cooked, cleaned and mostly kept to himself.

Except for when he was talking - this, by the way, was all the time. He would just never shut up. Every little thing that came to his mind, he would have either an opinion about or a tidbit of trivia to share with John. Watching TV with the DVR was a special kind of hell for John, especially if Dwayne had command of the remote control, which was always.

Because Dwayne was incarcerated for so long, he had had a lot of time to peruse the prison library's computer for movie web sites like Rotten Tomatoes and Imdb. There was blocking software on the prison computers so the inmates couldn't surf porn, but Hollywood movies were the next best thing. The movie web sites had samples and trailers from films and TV shows. Dwayne was able to watch and track down all of his favorite television and movie actors and characters through simple site searches.

There he would find page upon page of information and

message boards about the various players. So every time an actor he was familiar with appeared on the TV screen, Dwayne would freeze the frame and tell John a story about the actor. And Dwayne knew his stuff. Little details about each individual's life that most wouldn't be aware of.

That's why John had gone to Larry at Dink's Diner at closing time a few days after Dwayne had arrived, to ask if the dishwasher's job was still available. John was more pleading than asking, and it had its desired effect.

Dwayne started working at Dink's the following day. If he could keep quiet about living at John's house, he would be able to keep the job as long as he worked up to Lou's expectations.

Larry didn't want to jeopardize his own job, knowing Lou hated John, by letting slip that Dwayne was bunking with the source of Lou's disdain.

Dwayne, although only in the dishwasher's position for a day or so, loved it. He'd become quite proficient in the State Pen's kitchen, enjoying his time alone early in the mornings making homemade bread.

Most of the prison food was barely edible, but the administrators of the Kentucky prison system learned early on that it was more cost-effective to bake their own bread. The flour was inexpensive when purchased in bulk, and the ample supply of cheap labor sealed the deal.

First smelling and ultimately sampling the crusty bread each and every day was one of the only legal pleasures the inmates got enjoyment from.

Dwayne doubly liked his time alone with the dough-making process. And although the Dink's Diner kitchen was pretty small, it was well-appointed. Dwayne knew all about the various kitchen appliances and implements.

Larry was, at first, impressed by Dwayne's knowledge and conversely annoyed with him for talking so fucking much about it all. Larry made several mental notes to give John some shit about it later.

CHAPTER
- 30 -

Jimmy the cop couldn't believe his bad luck that morning. First his car wouldn't start and he was late for work, and once on the job, his first report of the day was a yuppie transplant couple from California who couldn't quite bring themselves to fully explain their problem.

The California couple spoke with an advanced vocabulary, but they kept circling back to where they began without making a point that Jimmy could decipher. But finally, after picking up enough information through the couple's stop and start sentences, Jimmy was slowly piecing together a story about trusting adults and confused teenagers.

Finally, Jimmy thought that it all had jelled. "You think someone's messing with your teenage daughter?" he said.

"It's our son, Danny, officer," said Sharon.

And as Danny's parents explained in further detail, Jimmy had to do his best acting job not to let on that he was silently seething. How could his brother, John, be so stupid as to get involved in the California couple's creepy kid's life?

He knew who Danny was. Every cop on the Balmoral police

force knew who he was because the kid had had a verbal run-in with every single one of them.

To date, Danny hadn't done anything they could charge him with, but he stood out among the other area youth. It was more the way the kid interacted with others that brought him so much attention, not so much his raggedy attire. Jimmy had two words in mind when envisioning Danny: douche bag.

As Sharon and Donald continued, Jimmy was filtering their conversation for any phrases that would incriminate his brother, but he was using most of his brain remembering back to when John was a teenager himself. He thought about the way John interacted with others during his youth. What he could remember, anyway, from the few times he interacted with his brother during his teenage years.

Jimmy thought of the way John dressed and acted back in the day, all the Goth clothing and dyed, black hair. He came to the conclusion that he could understand perfectly why his younger brother would be interested in a kid like Danny. They were kindred spirits.

"Is there a reward?"

Jimmy's filter kicked in, "A reward? A reward for what exactly, sir?"

Donald didn't want to go into detail with Jimmy, but the bottom line was that he needed the money. His employer had relocated his family from San Mateo, California, to Balmoral a year before, and just this week, they informed him that his pay would be cut 20 percent to make up for the lowered cost of living expenses in Illinois.

By the look on Sharon's face after Donald asked if a reward was available, Jimmy knew that she and her husband were on separate pages when it came to their family's welfare and, apparently, finances.

Just as Sharon was about to protest to her husband on where this entire conversation was heading, she finally noticed Jimmy's nameplate.

Sgt. Caul.

"I think we've taken up too much of your time, officer," she said. "I'm sure this is all nothing, and we're just being overprotective parents."

She pulled the confused Donald to his feet and gently pushed him toward the door of the police department.

CHAPTER
- 31 -

She had followed him for two straight days. She watched carefully, she thought, from a distance, as he strolled from one place to the next, always turning back to Dink's Diner for his meals. It was the only place in town where she couldn't follow.

She retraced his route, going inside the businesses he had just walked out of, asking the people inside of the various establishments what the man had asked them. The townsfolk she encountered were as confused by her questions as his. But slowly, she was able to glean that the man was asking about a guy named John whose brother was a cop in town.

When he again stepped into Dink's Diner, she had to wait across the street and out of view inside the Superstar's Coffee Shop. She couldn't chance going inside the diner because she would be exposed the minute she stepped foot in the door.

It would happen when her brother-in-law, Lou, would see and warmly greet her. She loved Lou like her own brother, and she just couldn't chance being seen. Not until she was able to clear her son, Tyler, of the trouble he had wrought upon himself.

But something worse than being found out by her family had

taken place, and now she found herself in the cheap motel room on Route 14 waiting for him. She was trapped. Not physically, but emotionally, by his blackmail.

She had only been with one man for the past 20 years, and the thought of even being with the paunchy and slimy Enright sickened her, but Rita knew she had to go through with the blackmailed tryst or else Tyler would be exposed as a stalker and likely killer in the making. His life would be ruined before it even really started.

The man grabbed her by the elbow as she stepped from the Superstar's Coffee Shop. He spun her around, leading them both toward the train station, telling her to smile and nod, as if nothing was wrong or else he'd hurt her. She complied.

She had lost sight of him when he went into Dink's this last time, but as soon as he grabbed her elbow, she knew she had made an enormous mistake by taking up a viewing position in Superstar's Coffee Shop where only one of the two doors at Dink's was visible.

He obviously had stepped out the side door and worked his way around the back side of the diner and across Balmoral Road out of her field of vision.

She finally stopped walking just shy of the train station parking lot, and pulled her arm free.

"I know what you're doing and you have to stop!" Rita said.

It was her only purpose in this endeavor. Her only mission in following Enright was to stop the madness that her 17-year-old son, Tyler, had started.

"We should go somewhere private and talk it through, babe," said Enright with a greasy smile.

And now here she sat for the past two hours on the edge of the creaky bed in room 115 of the cheap motel on Route 14 just outside of Balmoral awaiting her sexual fate.

In an odd way, though, it would be worth it for the man to stop working for her son. She could resolve to forgive herself for this sin against the 20-year relationship with the man she truly loved.

It would all work out.

***

Enright pulled his crappy car in front of the cheap motel on Route 14, exited his vehicle and made his way to room 115, his head on a swivel making sure no one was following.

Working as a PI had sharpened his skill of making sure he never picked up tails. He employed those skills when he noticed Rita following him. He knew she was there ten minutes after she started her amateurish surveillance the day before. But he was biding his time, making sure he'd confront her when she least expected it.

And now he was heading to room 115 for a little something-something to warm up and change the pace of his day. He had no intention of stopping his investigation of John Caul and his brother Jimmy the cop. He knew they were probably working together in the Baby Face Robber scheme. Jimmy was probably acting as the setup man, researching the best places to hit, and John did the actual robbing. He was not going to stop because he was so close to snagging the robbery proceeds all for himself.

And he was going to blackmail Tyler's father, too.

Rita was a total bonus. Hell, he thought, he'd extort cash from her as well after he partook of other pleasures. Enright was sure that a woman as pampered as Rita could cough up some nice dough of her own. This was turning out to be a damned good day's work for Enright.

But Enright's reverie was misguided. His internal radar was excellent at picking one tail, but not multiple tails.

Right at that very moment, across the street parked in his car, sat Lou. He had his chrome-plated .357 revolver resting in his lap.

CHAPTER
- 32 -

John pushed aside a heavy, green canvas bag containing baseball bats, and he pulled up the loosened floor boards of the park's equipment shack.

There, tightly wrapped in heavy-duty, clear plastic, were the large Vicodin bottles and the remainder of the cash proceeds from his robbing activities.

Although Brick had threatened his life during their last meeting, John had once again contacted the drug dealer asking if he was more interested this time in actually purchasing the drugs than killing him. Brick was and they set up a meeting.

Brick, still shaken from their last get-together, proposed that they'd meet at the Schaumburg Police Department parking lot. It was neutral ground for both. John countered that they both should come alone this time.

"We gotta talk."

John dropped the floorboards and spun to see Danny standing in the doorway of the shack. The kid nodded his head to the side, motioning John from the tiny building. It appeared to John that the teen hadn't seen what he was doing with the floorboards, so he played it cool and followed him outside.

"Look, I'm sorry you had to see what I was doing. I didn't want anyone to know until after," John said, stopping himself from going any further. But added, "I know I frightened you and I'm sorry about that."

Danny just stared at John so John measured his words very carefully. "I know you haven't said anything to the police, or your parents for that matter, so I'll tell you what I'm doing. The reason I'm doing all of this. The baby face stuff, you know."

John went on to explain about his years of being used as a scapegoat by the townspeople and his idea of finally bringing shame to those who had given him so much grief over the years.

He explained that now, as he became more and more Vicodin-free, he realized that the drug had skewed his thought process in the entire affair. But he was still holding to his plan the best he could.

Danny listened quietly so John went on to explain why he had shown an interest in Danny – because they were more alike than the teen realized. John said, "I don't want to see you travel the same path as me."

After John had finished his verbal vomiting, Danny said, "I'm not afraid, jerk off. I want to go with you next time."

When John's expression froze in place, Danny added, "That's right, fuck-stick, we rob someone soon or else I will talk. I'll tell fucking everyone. The celebration will never be saved. And you won't be able to fuck the town over."

***

Tyler eyed John and Danny from his car in the McDonald's parking lot. His mother's behavior was extremely odd of late and that precipitated his actions in following her and seizing onto John's trail.

Rita had taken to leaving Tyler to watch his little brother, Christopher, while she "ran errands." He knew that she was up to no good, so he took to following her. He soon discovered that she was tracking Enright.

Instead of following in both Enright's and his mother's footsteps, he simply used his extra car key to rummage through Rita's car when she was following Enright. That's where he found the simple note on the pad of paper on her front seat that read: Name is John. Lady in cupcake shop says he's the brother of Balmoral cop, Jimmy Caul.

It didn't take long to figure out where John Caul lived. He just called 411 from his cell phone while his brother napped in his car seat in the back of his Jeep Cherokee.

For the past day, he'd been watching John's house on Coleridge Avenue, following his prey whenever he left in the old station wagon. Tyler hid the 12 gauge shotgun in the back of his Jeep under a battered sleeping bag. When the moment was right, and he didn't have his little brother with him, he would shoulder his way into John's home and take care of his father's problem. It would be loud. It would be bloody and ugly. But it would be done.

CHAPTER
- 33 -

It was a slow lunch rush at Dink's Diner so Lou told Dwayne he was done for the afternoon. Larry would be able to cook and keep up with the dirty dishes.

It was a stunningly beautiful day so Dwayne took the long route when walking back to John's house. He was truly falling in love with the town of Balmoral. What was not to like? The area held that solid and quintessential, small-town feel but with an upscale twist.

Slowly strolling up and down the neatly manicured blocks, Dwayne had the feeling that he was on a Hollywood movie set. It looked like Bedford Falls in summertime. He thought that George Bailey could sprint past him at any moment calling out loudly about his love for the town.

He noticed that there were, indeed, some modern-looking homes where older homes obviously used to stand, but by the age of the newer homes, he discerned that the teardown craze had stopped about 15 years ago. That was when Balmoral had adopted a strict, historical district code for the homes in the area. Teardowns were forbidden from here on out. Looking at the older homes, some of which were probably candidates for a teardown/ rebuild scenario at some point, the homeowners, instead, had taken to rehabbing them with much care and expense.

Although surrounded by small-town beauty, a troubling thought was wriggling around deep in that reptilian portion of Dwayne's brain. It was a feeling that this life he was now living was artificial.

Sure, he was working a crappy gig as a dishwasher in a little diner, but still it was all too good to be true. He was a free man. Just a few weeks earlier he had woken for the last time in a dingy prison cell, said goodbye to the select few inmates and guards that he considered friends and had made his way to the area in search of his sister.

He was free to do what he wanted, within the law, but he couldn't help but feel that his freedom was a terrifying proposition. The idea that he was now totally in charge of every move he would make from here on out scared the shit out of him.

He had grown accustomed to being told where to go and what to do day in and day out for the past several years, but now there were no correctional officers to do his thinking for him. That's probably the reason that Dwayne was comfortable at Dink's Diner. Lou was very much like the guards at the state pen, telling him what to do and how to do it. That was the only small comfort in his life now.

And now, as he sat at John's kitchen table spilling his inner thoughts to Jimmy the cop, he felt relief for the first time in a few weeks. He had finally verbalized his feelings to someone he could trust.

Oddly enough, Dwayne and Jimmy had taken an instant liking to one another from the get-go. Okay, maybe not so instantaneously. Jimmy had drawn down on Dwayne with his Glock when he found him rummaging through the fridge at John's house, thinking he was a burglar.

After spotting the Semper Fi tattoo on Dwayne's forearm, though, Jimmy started talking instead of shooting. They were soon laughing when Jimmy discovered that the reason Dwayne had been drummed out of the Corps was due to the fact that he had knocked out an asshole sergeant who Jimmy was very familiar with. It was a guy that Jimmy himself once had a fight with after finding the offending sergeant stealing socks from his locker.

"That fucker stole everything that wasn't nailed down," said Dwayne. "I caught him once before and warned him, but he didn't like a boot telling him what to do. After he snagged some shaving cream from me, I knocked the sumbitch o-u-t."

Dwayne had done his time and didn't mind one little bit talking to a cop about his troubles. There was nothing Jimmy could do to him now. In fact, he felt more comfortable around Jimmy than anyone of his other new acquaintances and that included Lou. They were on opposite sides of the law, but they traveled in the same circles, so to speak.

"I'm not sure this freedom thing is worth it. A bud of mine in the pen was originally from Wisconsin. He said the food and bunks were much nicer there," said Dwayne. "I mean we're only a few miles from the Wisconsin border, right?" he added.

Jimmy smiled and said, "Don't go all 'recidivist' on me, Dwayne. If you can handle boot camp, you can make it in the world."

CHAPTER
- 34 -

John stood next to his old station wagon in the far rear portion of the Schaumburg police department parking lot, holding a large, steaming cup of coffee.

The coffee wasn't for drinking.

He still had not found a new gun for future robbing activities. The old gun was, indeed, picked up by the Fox River Grove police after the fiasco in the cornfield. The gun had no identifying marks or serial numbers on it anywhere, so he wasn't concerned that the Fox River Grove cops would pin the robberies on him.

In the past few days, he had taken to storing a baby face mask in the spare tire compartment in the rear of his station wagon, just in case he did find a gun and a place to take down at a moment's notice. It would go against the agreement he had made with Jimmy not to rob anyone for the time being, but he still thought he needed to be prepared.

Refocusing on the task at hand, John couldn't help but be leery of Brick. John was going to use the scolding coffee as a molten weapon if Brick chose not to be a gentleman.

Surprisingly, Brick was quite professional this time around.

Maybe even a bit contrite.

After pulling up in his Escalade - alone, as promised - the drug dealer apologized for how he had acted and offered an extra $5,000 for all the trouble he had caused.

John wouldn't be getting the $75,000 he knew the drugs were worth, but he was satisfied with the deal they had struck on the phone.

The exchange happened in the blink of an eye: one, large, brown paper bag from Brick to John and vice versa.

Brick said, "No need to count it. It's all there. I promise."

And John believed him.

Brick, without his minions to impress, was quite a charming young man. John thought that a guy like Brick would probably do well in any chosen profession.

"This is gonna help me with a start-up in Naperville."

"I'm starting a new company now, too," said John.

"You and those trigger men from your yard?" asked Brick.

"No, it's legitimate, a real business franchise."

"I'm not sure if I'm cut out for the legit shit, you know?" said Brick.

John studied the young man for a second or two, and said, "I bet you'd do just fine. They still have the franchise show going on at McCormick Place. You should check it out."

But John couldn't help launching a seemingly harmless, verbal jab at Brick to make sure no funny stuff would happen after the exchange went down, though.

He said, "What a coincidence that you offered to meet here at the Schaumburg PD."

Brick smirked and looked a question at John.

"That buddy of mine you met in my yard, you know, the one with the rifle pointed at your head? He's a cop here," John lied.

"I like you, man. I like the way you do shit. You're a cool dude, man," said Brick.

He stood staring, nodding and smiling at John.

"I'm glad we made peace, you know. I bet we could do shit

together in the future," he said. "I will check out that shit at McCormick Place. Good looking out, man."

John stepped towards his car $45,000 richer for his efforts. He got into his station wagon and took off.

Brick watched him go, but soon lost his grin as he scanned the windows of the Schaumburg PD making sure no one was watching. He got into his Escalade and drove away, heading toward Naperville to meet with his new business partner – the dentist - formerly of Lake Zurich, Illinois.

CHAPTER
- 35 -

Driving north on Balmoral Road, John was on a serious daydreaming jag.

He had $45,000 in the brown paper bag on the seat next to him and a new business venture in the works. He was picturing a location for the Kid Crew on heavily traveled Route 14. In that spot, the most eyeballs would be on the colorful signage that Henry and his late wife had created. He imagined that the walk-in business alone would be enough to keep him and Amy in the black.

He had been slowly stepping down from his Vicodin usage and his mind was incrementally becoming clearer as each hour passed. Instead of taking the high number he had been ingesting, admittedly sometimes 20 per day, John had quickly weaned himself down to 10 half pills a day.

He was able to accomplish that through sheer willpower. His withdrawal symptoms were still present - the nausea, jitters and shakes, as well as sweats - but he knew he had turned a corner and would be completely Vicodin-free in no time. So what if the searing pain in his back and hip had returned, at least his head was clear.

And as John's mind cleared, he found that he could link one thought to the next and solve problems instead of fixating on, and becoming obsessed with, only one issue, as he had done with trying to save the Fourth of July Festival. He still wanted to save the celebration, but new options were opening in his life, and he sought to explore all the positive opportunities that were coming his way – namely, Amy.

His daydreaming came to a sudden halt when a silver-colored Mercedes SUV took a perilous turn in front of him at the intersection of Balmoral and Dundee Roads. In a nanosecond, he was able to apply the brakes and identify the driver – Keith Michaels, the marmot-like, village council member - alone in the car.

Luckily, there was only one other car in back of John, a maroon Jeep Cherokee driven by a large, male teenager. The driver of the Cherokee was able to keep his distance and brake safely as John's station wagon screeched to a halt in the intersection. John pulled hard on the steering wheel, and the station wagon took off after the Mercedes.

When he caught up with the errant driver, John didn't tailgate. He simply followed eastbound on Dundee as Keith Michaels drove and carried on a very animated conversation with the cell phone pressed to his ear. Keith was obviously in a heated argument with the person on the other end of the line and hadn't noticed John tailing him.

When Keith couldn't cough up the $150,000 owed to his dangerous creditor (the initial $50,000 plus the additional $100,000 promised), Franky "Five Bucks" himself made it a habit of calling to cajole the councilman five or six times a day, doing his intimidating best to get Keith to pay back the money.

"You fuck. You take my money you pay me back!" screamed Franky "Five Bucks" in his choppy Chicago/Danish accent.

Franky sat in his Oak Park home and chewed on a delicate piece of apple kringle that he had purchased the week before during a trip to Racine. Franky made it a monthly habit of driving the few hours to Racine to pick up his favorite childhood treat. In his expert opinion, the Danes in Racine never lost the talent for baking the best kringle in America.

"I don't have your goddamned money. You'll have to give me more time," said Keith.

After a mile and a few more high-volume go-rounds of imploring Franky "Five Bucks" that he did not have all the money, Keith disconnected the call and tossed the cell phone onto the passenger seat and took a hard right into an upscale subdivision.

John followed and watched ahead as the Mercedes took a left into a cul-de-sac where only two homes stood, both of them enormous and worth well over a million dollars each.

John slowly drove past and looked left to see the SUV glide into an open garage, the door closing as soon as the car stopped. This confused John because he was no longer in Balmoral. He was in the suburb of Inverness, which was an entirely separate municipality.

Why would a Balmoral city councilman live in Inverness, unless Keith Michaels was just visiting someone and they allowed him to park in the garage?

John parked in the next cul-de-sac where two more similarly expensive homes stood, got out, walked to the rear of his car and opened the back door. He pulled back the carpet-covered section of cardboard that hid the spare tire, grabbed up the baby face mask hiding there and took off on foot back to where Keith had parked.

He palmed the mask and strolled painfully to the rear of the huge, brick home where the councilman had parked his car. His back spasms were growing more constant the past few days, and he had to stop twice to allow them to subside. But as he neared the backyard he could hear Keith's raised voice in a one-sided and heated argument.

John couldn't make out the exact words but money was mentioned three times so far. The day was warm and the home

Keith was standing in had the rear French doors open to the expanse of the backyard.

"Well, fuck you! I don't have it! What are you going to do?" yelled Keith into the cell phone, as John, the mask now covering his face, stepped into the house through the open French doors. Keith was so upset that he didn't even notice John standing five feet away.

John was not armed but he improvised and slid his hand to his lower back as Keith finally disconnected the cell call and noticed him standing an arm's length away.

"Oh! Fucking - what the hell?!"

"Take a breath, Keith. Relax," said John.

But Keith didn't relax. He made a move toward an open doorway in the study they currently stood in.

"Don't," was all John said. The tone worked, and Keith froze in place and turned back to facing the masked John.

"Franky sent you, didn't he?"

John looked about the room, noticing the framed photos everywhere. Hanging photos on the walls and standing framed photos were on every flat surface. Keith was in nearly every one of them.

"How can a Balmoral Village council member live in Inverness?" asked John.

Keith's shoulders finally relaxed, and he motioned toward a side board where a bottle of Johnny Walker Black and a few glasses were located. John nodded and Keith made himself a stiff drink. He took a long gulp -- and unloaded all of his troubles on John.

"If I'm dying today, I may as well confess my sins to someone, right?" he asked shakily.

And unload his burden he did.

John learned that the house was his in-laws. They purchased it with cash and gave it to his wife after being unimpressed with the fixer-upper that Keith had purchased and had been bleeding and sweating over as he tried to rehab it on his own for the past few years.

The house Keith purchased was located only four blocks from John's own home but in an area near the high school and the freight train tracks. The house was nice but less desirable in his in-laws' estimation. And it was a house not worthy of their daughter to live in.

John asked, "What about the new SUV?"

"It's leased…in my father-in-law's name. That son of a bitch didn't want his grandkids driving around in a Chevy. Fuck him, right?"

Keith didn't hold back because he assumed that John had been sent by Franky "Five Bucks" to kill him, so he told John all about the sordid, Randall Road land purchase details including how he had taken the money from his wife's account to try to get out from under his in-laws' thumb.

John wasn't sure how to continue, either. He didn't count on feeling sorry for this guy. He thought that Keith could be the one taking his robbery/Fourth of July proceeds, and he probably was, but how in the hell was he supposed to proceed in scaring the money out of him now?

John's plan, albeit quickly concocted on the short drive to this Inverness cul-de-sac, was simply to confront Keith and to try and get some of his money back.

John finally said, "You took the money from the wicker basket, didn't you?"

That's when Keith literally dropped the glass in his hand to the carpeted floor. Shortly after the glass bounced off the floor, Keith was kneeling right next to it – a completely beaten man.

Keith mumbled, "The Baby Face Robber. Oh, my God. I'm. I'm…I…"

John wasn't sure if he wanted to physically lash out at this man or not, but as he was thinking it through, a strange, whirring sound started, growing louder as it approached the study.

"What's that noise?" said John, reaching toward his back waistband again where his fake gun didn't reside.

"Please, don't. Please…"

And that's when Kenny Michaels, Keith's nine-year-old, quadriplegic son, rolled into the room in his breathing-tube guided electric chair.

"Is everything okay, daddy?"

Before Keith could answer, John was out the door jogging back to his car. The little boy never even saw him.

***

Keith Michaels never did call the police to report the strange meeting in his study with the Baby Face Robber. It would only complicate things for his family, and he wanted to keep his troubles quiet as long as he could.

That night, when he had regrouped and had dinner with his wife and children, he stepped out to the cul-de-sac to retrieve his mail. What he found along with a smattering of credit card offers was a tightly wrapped brown paper bag containing $45,000 in cash.

Keith hugged the money to his chest, sat on the driveway and wept.

CHAPTER
- 36 -

He was angry with himself as he pulled out of the Inverness subdivision, $45,000 lighter. He was so angry that he didn't even notice that he was being followed by the Jeep Cherokee.

Leaving the $45,000 behind was an impulsive reaction to Keith's dire financial and family situation. The poor mope needed the money more than he did, but he was still mentally kicking himself in the ass on the rest of the car ride to the Route 14 area.

While driving towards Balmoral Road and Route 14, John had driven past an empty storefront that was, at one time, a carpet wholesale store. With 20-foot-high, wall-to-wall and floor-to-ceiling glass facing the street, it would be perfect for the Kid Crew franchise location.

Literal transparency would be a boon for this particular business franchise, because passing motorists would be able to peer inside and see the goings-on as the children skittered about – tumbling, dancing, and generally having a good time.

And what made that even more appealing was that it was only two blocks from the busy Route 14 and Balmoral Road intersection. Most weekdays during the morning and evening rush hours, the cars in either direction would be slowed to a crawl. That meant even more wandering eyeballs on the Kid Crew franchise.

John had made a few runs, driving back and forth past the empty storefront trying to get a feel for where he should place the signage. His mind wandered, though, now coming to the conclusion that he was going to have to dip back into his money market funds to complete the build-out of the franchise.

He made his decision to help Keith Michaels, and now he was moving forward, putting the negative thoughts of losing the $45,000 behind him. He had to if he wanted to make any of this work in order to get on Amy's good side. And really, who was he kidding - neither the Vicodin nor the $45,000 he received for selling it was his anyway.

John pulled his car onto a side street and maneuvered a quick U-turn, ready to drive past the empty storefront once more. But he was instantly yanked from his daydreaming by the sight of Lou, the Dink's Diner owner, armed with a .357 revolver in hand, stepping from his car and angling across the rear parking lot of the cheap motel.

John knew that Lou was a miserable human being, but he didn't like seeing anyone in this much distress. The man looked like he was on the verge of tears. John screeched his car to a halt, cutting Lou off from the building.

Lou knew in his heart that Rita was not willingly waiting in the room. He had watched as Enright left his diner and caught up to, and surprised, Rita outside the Superstar's Coffee Shop. He sensed immediately they were not friends.

Growing up in Greece, he knew plenty of operators like Enright - guys always angling for more, always on the take, always looking to screw someone over for their own gain.

Lou had followed Rita, after Enright left her near the train station, to the cheap motel. The moment she stepped up to room 115 with a long face, he knew she was not here of her own accord.

And now he was so focused on the murderous task of taking

Enright out that it took him a full two seconds before he could recognize that it was John who had stopped him in his tracks, jumped from the old station wagon and disarmed him.

"You fuck! Give me gun."

"Lou, what's going on? What are you doing?"

"Taking care of my family. Now give me gun!"

Both men froze when they heard the distinct sound of a shotgun wracking a round into the chamber.

"Uncle Lou, step away," said Tyler as he pointed the shotgun at John's left ear.

"Tyler, why you do this? What's the matter?" said Lou.

"Hi, Tyler. Nice to meet you," was all John could muster as he looked, literally, down the barrel of the massive gun.

"Shut the hell up, man. I know what you did. You ruined him. He's never gonna be the same."

Lou took a small step toward his nephew and said, "Please, give me the gun. You don't want to hurt this man."

"He's the one, Uncle Lou. He's the guy who robbed pop's place – he's the Baby Face Robber."

Lou slowly turned toward John, his face contorting in anger. John, in total surrender, carefully handed the .357 revolver back to Lou. "I don't know what he's talking about," said John sheepishly.

"All he does now is look at the walls, man. You fucked him up!" said Tyler as he edged even closer to John. John closed his eyes awaiting his fate.

"Tyler!"

John opened an eye to see a pretty woman in her thirties running at full sprint toward the muscular teenager. Tyler faltered and lowered the gun just an inch.

"Put that away," said Rita, finally noticing her other son Christopher sleeping in the maroon Jeep. "What is wrong with you?"

"What's wrong with me? Why in the hell are you following Enright? Huh, mom? I hired him to find this dude so I could kill him. You know what he did to our family!"

"Mom?" said John.

"Honey, you'll ruin your entire life. Please, this has gone too far. Put it down. Give it to me."

Tyler raised the gun again – ready to take John's head off. John didn't close his eyes, but he did smirk.

"What so funny," said Lou.

John nodded to the other side of the parking lot. Jimmy aimed his AR-15 rifle from across the hood of his Balmoral Police cruiser. "Let's all drop 'em. Drop 'em now!" said Jimmy.

***

Enright had seen enough to prove that his hypothesis about John being the Baby Face Robber and his cop brother, Jimmy, working as his accomplice was spot on.

Through a two-inch-wide gap in the curtains of room 115, he could see it all play out. The crazy, diner owner with his chrome-plated cannon in hand, the hulking teenager pointing the shotgun at John's head, the kid's mom, who had rushed from the same room just moments before he could wet his wick, pleading with her kid to put the gun away. And now the Balmoral copper ready to take them all down with one short burst from the AR-15 in his hands. It cemented all of his work up to this point.

Enright knew exactly where John lived, and with everyone tied up in the parking lot, he made his exit through the small bathroom window, squeezing his bulk through the opening and scurrying on foot toward Coleridge Avenue to see if he could locate some of the robbery proceeds. He'd deal with the mother and the restaurant owner later. From his past experiences, blackmail, most times, was best served lukewarm.

CHAPTER
- 37 -

Enright jogged past the BMW dealership, where inside, Mr. James, the manager, now sporting two black eyes from the broken nose Amy provided him, was showing a new 5-series to an athletic looking 40-year-old man. Mr. James pointed at Enright as he moved past the front windows.

"So, yeah, she pops me in the nose. Broke it, too. But that's not the weirdest part of my week. A few days later I get that guy right there coming in asking all sorts of questions. Thought he was a cop like you."

Mr. James noticed the uncomfortable expression that the man shot his way. He read from the police badge attached to his belt loop under his sport jacket.

"Paladin PD, huh? So that guy…I thought he was a…police officer."

"What was he asking?" said the Paladin officer, a guy named Shane Thompson, as he tried to get a look at Enright, who was completely out of view now.

"Kept asking about the Baby Face Robber."

This spun Thompson on his heels, his interest and piercing

eyes all on Mr. James. "Baby Face Robber? What did he want to know from you? Tell me exactly."

Mr. James was a little fearful of Thompson now. "He asked if there was anyone in Balmoral who I thought could do something stupid."

"Stupid? Like rob a place?"

"Actually, he asked if I were to think of one name right off the top of my head of anyone in town who could be the Baby Face Robber, who would that be? So I told him."

***

Danny was chilling on a bench when he saw all the shit going down at the cheap motel bordering the park.

The fat, older dude squeezing out of the small, bathroom window made him laugh out loud, it was that comical. He watched as the fat dude jogged toward town. He knew that he came from the room where the dark-haired lady had gone earlier.

Once Jimmy the cop had pulled that big automatic rifle on the group in the back parking lot, things settled rather quickly. The big kid, who was about Danny's age, had placed the shotgun on the ground, and the guy who owned the diner had done the same with his revolver.

Jimmy had lowered his gun and gathered all the players into a circle to converse. What Danny thought could become an action packed scenario, complete with shots fired at close range, had quickly deescalated into a regular old conversation. B-o-r-i-n-g.

Danny decided that there may be more action in following the fat, older dude who was now moving past the BMW dealership, so he paralleled Route 14 on a side street and shadowed the guy.

As they came to the town's center, Danny had the sinking feeling that the guy was heading to John's house. That would make sense since he first noticed the guy when he was following John earlier in the week. Was he a cop? Was John about to get arrested? Was Danny's chance of robbing someone with the Baby Face Robber going down in flames?

The fat, older dude kept walking south on Balmoral toward Coleridge, so Danny took a right on Trussell and sprinted to Lilly where he took a left.

As Enright quickstepped toward the intersection of Coleridge and Lilly, he was smacked square in the face with a thick mud ball. By the time the surprise and initial sting wore off, Enright could see Danny standing a few houses away. There was a running water hose snaked between his feet, and he was holding yet another mud ball.

"Hey, fuck-stick! Nice face," said Danny, laughing.

Enright, wiped the gritty mud from his left eye and immediately gave chase. Danny waited until Enright was within 30 feet before he turned and took off back toward Trussell.

Danny kept going west on Trussell toward Dundee. As he neared the intersection, he saw John's car, followed by a maroon Jeep and Jimmy the cop in his police car – all of them driving past on Dundee heading toward John's house.

Enright saw the same thing and broke off the chase, did a U-turn and headed toward John's house back the way he came. Danny stopped and walked to a house mid-block and snuck his way through the yard to get a vantage point on John's house.

By the time Danny got into a viewing position, and had his eyes on John's place, he could see Enright sneak into the garage and out of view. John and the rest of the people formerly at the cheap motel, stepped from their various cars and walked into John's house through the front door.

***

Enright moved with cautious purpose, opening cabinets, and drawers in the garage, hoping to find something incriminating that would solidify his hunch about John. He could hear raised voices, mostly the Greek guy who owned the diner, coming from the house. But every time the Greek raised his voice, he could also hear a low and measured reply by the one he knew as John.

Enright inched toward the window on the side of the garage

and could just get a glimpse of John, palms out, speaking in a calm manner to the others in attendance in his kitchen.

Enright went back to opening any storage area he could, including the large freezer positioned in the corner of the garage. The freezer was stocked full of frozen pizza boxes, but he couldn't find anything other than normal, garage items elsewhere. As he leaned against the freezer, though, he caught a glimpse of something made of clear plastic peeking from its hiding place above the cabinets.

His hopes were raised as he reached up and came back down holding a baby face mask.

CHAPTER
- 38 -

It was the first he had heard about the problem with the high school gym's foundation and how it was in need of urgent repair.

The old-timers, especially Emil, were speaking in hushed tones about the topic at hand, but made sure every so often to raise their voices loud enough so that John would hear.

John knew what they were doing. It was the old-timers way of saying "If you hadn't burned down the old place with its fortress of a foundation, we wouldn't be having this problem now."

John's head was nearly 100 percent clear. The back and hip pain was searing, but this new clarity also helped with his fading intent on embarrassing the Balmoral townspeople. As John breakfasted in Dink's Diner, free of Lou's disapproving looks and remarks, he was much more attuned to the goings-on around him.

"You didn't guess," said Larry.

"Raw garlic? No, roasted garlic."

"You're good, man," said Larry, heading back into the kitchen where Dwayne was doing dishes. John finished up his meal, stood and stepped toward Lou who was standing at the front register. Lou didn't quite smile, but he didn't sneer, either; he just nodded for John to go – breakfast was on the house.

Larry and Dwayne saw the exchange between Lou and John from the kitchen pass-through. Larry shrugged to Dwayne, and Dwayne went back to scrubbing over-easy egg yolks off of plates.

***

Before driving to the high school to witness for himself the waning foundation situation, John had driven, first, past the Athenian in Paladin or Arlington Heights or wherever. Next he slowly rolled past the spa with the fake-sounding, French name in that wide-arching Lifestyle Center in Deer Park.

Along with his clearer mind, regret was also churning deep in the recesses of John's brain. An hour and a half later, he found himself walking through the lobby of the upscale hotel in Lake Geneva.

He had to drive past and stop into each and every place he had robbed to see if the people inside each business were getting back to normal. He wanted to make sure that he hadn't permanently damaged anyone.

And by the looks of things at each place, everything was moving along just fine. The only place he was unable to confirm that life hadn't gone on as normal was at the dentist's office in Lake Zurich. That office seemed to have closed up overnight. There was no sign of life in the darkened building. Even the dentist's name had been scraped from the glass door.

But now, parked in the massive parking lot of Balmoral High School, shadowed by the equally enormous football stadium, John could only stare in silence.

Road hazard horses had been placed all around the gymnasium building keeping people away. A hard hat-wearing engineer stood next to the building making notes on a clipboard. As another engineer stepped towards the first one, they both spoke and made grand hand gestures, as if describing the way the entire building would cascade to the ground if one more crack formed in the weakening foundation.

That's when John drove away, heading toward the old carpet store on Route 14. He had an appointment with the owner about leasing the building for his Kid Crew venture.

***

"I'll need a year's payment up front," said Jer, the owner of the old carpet store. "And proof of insurance before we sign a lease. Can't have you backsliding on me, Sparky. Can't afford it."

John let the Sparky epitaph go, as he began writing a check.

Jer cleared his throat and said, "Cash."

John tucked his checkbook back into his pants pocket and nodded. As John walked from the store, Jer called after him, "My brother-in-law's an insurance agent, I'm sure he'd love to help you with the property insurance policy. I'll give him a call while you're getting the rent."

Jer had a sweetheart deal going with his alcoholic brother-in-law, the insurance man. Jer would get a 20 percent kickback on any policy he sent his brother-in-law's way and in return, his drunken brother-in-law would be free to carouse with the similarly alcoholic ladies he met and had trysts with at the roadhouses along rural Route 14. Several of the trysts Jer had witnessed himself as he, himself, was canoodling with the ladies.

And as part of this agreement, Jer promised that the brother-in-law's wife, Jer's sister, would never find out about any of it. It was a win-win situation for all involved.

Jer waited patiently inside the empty storefront while John went to the bank in town and came back with a stack of bills to pay the year's rent. But as John was about to hand over the stacks of cash, he pulled them back.

Jer was confused and asked, "Hey, we had a deal."

"We will, once you sign off on allowing me to double the size of the roadside signage," said John. He added, "You know, and I know that this new business will succeed if enough eyes see the sign."

John held the cash just out of Jer's reach. It didn't take all that long to consider.

"Do whatever you want," said Jer as John handed him the dough.

After they both signed the lease agreement, Jer told John to take his time getting the insurance certificate to him. He knew he was good for it now. Jer handed John the keys, stuffed the cash into his jacket pockets and left.

As John locked up the newly-leased Kid Crew location, someone honked the horn of their car just once. John turned and his heart sank.

Parked next to his old station wagon was a white Land Rover just like the one he saw Danny operating. But as he stepped to his car, he noticed that a woman was behind the wheel and the driver's window was down. She opened the door and swung her legs around as if about to get out of the vehicle.

"Hi, John. I'm Sharon, Danny's mom."

"Right. How are you?"

But before Sharon could answer, John got a visual reply. Sharon sat in the driver seat of her Land Rover wearing a revealing tank top and a short skirt that was hiked up to its highest logical place. The buttoned-down look she sported at her home the first time he had met her was no more. Even her demeanor seemed more relaxed. And by way of an answer to John's question, she did finally say, "Hop in."

Sharon hatched this plan after knowing that going through the police to investigate John would be a dead end, especially with Jimmy on the case.

She knew right away that it was an ill-advised strategy from the start. But she had to know if there was something reprehensible going on between John and her son, Danny. And the more she obsessed about the troubles her son was having, she couldn't help but think that her own personal relationship problems needed attention as well.

Donald hadn't touched her in a few months, and she craved attention - male attention. Even now, it was utterly confusing to her, and she wasn't sure when her plan went from saving her son from difficulty to getting into a bit of erotic trouble of her own, but here she was.

She was an incredibly sexy woman, maybe not in a Victoria's Secret model manner, but in that relaxed, intelligent-woman-who-knows-exactly-what-she-wants-from-life sort of way.

John really wasn't interested in what Sharon was selling. All he could think about was his dwindling bank accounts and trying to get the Kid Crew business off the ground. He was truly more focused on the need to keep Amy interested in him than anything else, though.

What he said was, "I really…can't. I'm sorry."

John thought it was enough to politely rebuke her advances, but he was wrong. She really wanted what she wanted. She quickly hopped out of the car, pushed John back against the old station wagon, leaned in and kissed him deeply.

As they separated, John said, "I can't." And he turned, got into his car and drove away.

Sharon's dreamy sexuality faded quickly as her anger took over. No one had ever turned her down - ever.

CHAPTER

- 39 -

In the kitchen area of the Athenian restaurant after the lunch rush had dwindled, it took several go-rounds of explanation before Jason settled down enough to truly understand what his brother, Lou, and his son, Tyler, were telling him.

And now, for the first time since robbing Jason of $1,200, John was back inside the restaurant, looking repentant and carrying a small, brown paper bag.

"Why should I not kill him here right now?" said Jason.

So Lou tried again with, "Because, brother, John helped us. He helped our family. Do you not understand?"

Lou didn't want to explain the part about his wife, Rita, almost being forcibly raped through a blackmail scheme by the sleazy Enright, though. He'd keep that from both Tyler, who wasn't aware even though he was there, and his younger brother, Jason. It would just hurt them too much to know.

John extended the small, brown paper bag to Jason, and said, "It's yours."

But Jason didn't accept it. Instead his eyes scanned the kitchen looking for a sharp implement to impale John with.

"I told you. I told you if I catch you that I'd kill you slowly," Jason said.

John, even though in real danger, did not back down. He pushed the bag into Jason's hands. Jason was so angry and frustrated, he looked as if he was either going to lash out physically or cry. He finally opened the bag and peered inside. He reached into the bag full of hundred dollar bills and gave them a cursory count.

"Don't understand. There's more than $3,000 here," he said.

The amount was $3,600 to be exact. John had counted them twice to make sure.

John said, "We'll say you loaned me the initial money, and I'm paying you back with interest. I'm truly sorry for what I put you and your family through."

But Jason wanted blood, and Lou and Tyler could tell.

Finally, Tyler stepped between his father and John and softly spoke to Jason. "Dad, I wanted to kill him. I almost did it, but his brother stopped me. His brother's a cop."

Jason's eyes fluttered and he finally looked Tyler in the eye, so Tyler continued, "His brother was going to arrest me, Pops, but John talked him out of it."

Lou added, "No one will know, brother. Tyler is not in trouble, and John is sincere in his apology. Please accept it."

Jason sent John a murderous glare, his mind wandering to how he had been visualizing this moment and how it would play out. It was a scenario that had run through his thoughts a hundred times a day since he'd been robbed and his dignity had been stripped bare.

He always imagined finding the Baby Face Robber, alone as he stepped from his green Saturn on a darkened, dead end street. That's how Jason had seen the vision in his deadly daydream.

Jason wouldn't use a gun, but would disarm the robber with a large aluminum baseball bat. A quick strike to the shoulder, and the 9mm in the masked man's hand would tumble to the ground. Jason would kick the gun from the area of operation and toss the bat aside, using his bare hands for the remainder of the wet work. He imagined beating the robber in the face repeatedly with his clenched fist while calmly voicing his disdain for the perpetrator.

Jason would let the robber know what he had done to him, to his family, to his business and how it would never go back to being the same.

After enough blood was spilled from the robber's face, Jason would firmly wrap his thick fingers around the neck of the now unmasked man. He'd slowly squeeze the life out of the man who had ruined his life.

And as most fantasies go, the locations tend to change at a moment's notice – so after the robber was no longer breathing, Jason always saw himself dragging the body to the quaint Town of Maine Cemetery on Touhy Avenue in Park Ridge, only two blocks from his home, where an already completed grave had been dug.

In his fantasy, he'd kick the body into the grave, and in a blink of an eye, the hole would be filled in and covered with fresh grass. Jason would be immediately clean of blood and dirt - smiling as he sat down for dinner in his home with his beautiful family.

His problem would be solved and he could go on with his life. That's how Jason had continuously fantasized about taking care of the Baby Face Robber.

But in reality, it took another few minutes of apologetic go-rounds between John, Tyler, Lou and Jason, before Jason finally calmed down enough to fix his stare again on John and ask, "You like blueberry pancakes?"

Jason finally hugged Tyler, and they both shuddered with a mixture of joy and relief.

CHAPTER
- 40 -

The train ride into the city of Chicago from Balmoral was a pleasant one, or so he thought. John gestured to points of interest along the way from their comfortable seats, and Amy pretended to be interested in what John had to say about the various bits of trivia he spouted.

"Robert Reed from the Brady Bunch grew up in that house right there," he said as they passed through Des Plaines.

"Park Ridge was originally called Brickton because of all the brick manufacturing companies located there at one time," he continued.

She had made a mistake when befriending John.

It actually gnawed at her from the moment they met, but she had been so desperate to find a job, start a career and begin a new life. What it mostly boiled down to, though, was that Amy was emotionally kicking herself for allowing another man to prescribe her life and future for her.

John was handsome and gentlemanly enough, and he was helping her brother, but he still had too much baggage.

She had done just a cursory bit of recon of John and his

existence after they became more involved in the Kid Crew venture. What she learned was that John had a history in Balmoral of being an outcast, and possibly a dangerous one, too.

She found out about the fire at the high school and how the locals never believed his story of how it was all an accident. Even though she wound up asking fifteen different people in town about John, they all had the same story about her new business partner.

Amy knew, first hand, that he was kicking a drug habit, as well, and that was the final straw. She had to figure out a way to both keep the job of running the Kid Crew franchise, something she truly wanted to do, and of dissuading John from pursuing her romantically.

She felt like a fraud for proceeding this way, but she really needed the job, just not John as a love interest. She needed to work on her own life before allowing another man into it.

She owed that to herself.

And really, if John knew what she was truly thinking, he would totally understand. But she couldn't chance him knowing the full truth. So she played along in a way. Not overtly with affection, because that would absolutely not be her style, but with faux interest in everything John had to say.

"Brickton, huh? Because of the bricks. That's interesting…"

Departing the Ogilvie Transportation Center on Madison Avenue in downtown Chicago, John and Amy, each carrying an overnight bag, took a brisk stroll to the State Street corporate offices of the Kid Crew. As they waited for the light to change at Clark Street, John gently took Amy's hand in his.

She didn't instantly pull away, but after the light changed, and they stepped forward, she made a move to pass a slower walker and dropped John's grasp.

John never tried to take her hand for the remainder of the short walk, and they soon found themselves riding in an elevator to the fifth floor of a 20-story building.

There they stepped directly into the lobby of the Kid Crew

corporate offices. The colorful signage was placed on the wall behind the reception desk, but the desk itself was empty. John cleared his throat, and both he and Amy could hear someone stepping quickly down a hall towards them.

"Hey, there they are!" said Henry, truly happy to see Amy more than John. He added, "Ready to hit the books?"

And the books they hit.

They studied the Kid Crew from the ground up. In the first eight hours of instruction, John and Amy were shown the proper bookkeeping techniques, schematics and photos of the correct layouts for the retail outlets and much more.

They learned that the kids they'd be dealing with were never to be spoken of as customers, or children, or kids, but as "crew members."

During one of the hourly, five-minute breaks, John made his way to the men's room and had to walk past the reception area.

He noticed, again, that the reception desk was empty. His curiosity got the best of him and he sidestepped the men's room to walk down the hallway to the other side of the office suites.

There John found one empty office after another. Some of the offices looked like they hadn't been used in a long time.

"I wasn't really trying to hide this, John. I hope you believe me," said Henry, now standing in the hallway near one of the empty offices.

"Kid Crew is real, isn't it?" asked John.

"It's a real business, but we've had a tough time keeping an administrative and marketing team. I've been doing everything myself. We have all the franchise locations that are listed in our marketing material, you can check for yourself."

John was now mentally kicking himself for not doing that before he sank his original money into this venture or renting the building on Route 14.

As John surveyed the empty offices, he made sure Amy wasn't hearing any of this. He stepped into the reception area and looked down the other hallway, where he could see her reading from one of the manuals Henry had given them.

"She can't hear us. I turned up the radio," said Henry. He added, "I do need another $10,000, though, John. I hate doing this to you, but if I can get that money, I'll be able to give this excellent franchise business developer I know the signing bonus he's requiring to start. If I can get him on board, I'll be able to raise the capital to staff the offices again. You know all those donut shop and ice cream store combinations you see everywhere now, he's the brains behind that."

"And if I don't?" asked John.

Henry wanted to speak but his eyes watered up, and he shrugged his shoulders a little instead.

"Shit," was all John could muster.

***

Amy was energized as they stepped out onto State Street from their first day of instruction with Henry.

She said, "I never thought learning about Excel spreadsheets could be so entertaining. Henry's a fantastic teacher, don't you think?"

John wasn't paying a lick of attention to Amy, though. His eyes were on the building across the street, where, in the lobby, a bank branch was located.

She asked absently, "Do you think he's seeing anyone?"

"Um, what?"

Amy couldn't believe she let that slip. "So, the hotel is a walk or a cab ride?"

John kept his eye on the busy bank branch.

His eyes scanned the wall-to-wall and floor-to-ceiling glass front, and the double door placement on the facade. The teller's counter was an L-shaped affair with six positions, but had only two tellers stationed there now. Neither of them were doing a whole lot of work. They looked bored in the otherwise empty bank.

John's eyes swiveled to the alleyway next to the bank

building itself. The front door of the bank was only five paces to the alley opening.

Shifting back to the bank he observed that there was no visible guard on duty.

He shook the thoughts flooding his head away, turned to Amy while sporting a forced grin and said, "The hotel is just around the corner. A couple of blocks at the most."

***

"The master bedroom is to the right, and the guest room is to the left," said the smartly-dressed bellman with the perfect teeth and blonde highlights.

John slipped him a twenty.

"Are you sure you don't want me to bring the bags into the master bedroom?" asked the bellman.

Amy looked a bit stricken and confused by the hotel room situation. The hotel suite was beautiful, very posh and modern, and she knew they'd be staying the night, but John had told her that they'd have separate rooms.

"Here's fine, thanks," said John.

"Mr. Caul, when you're ready for the dinner preparation, just press "zero" on the hotel phone, and the chef and his team will head on up. You have a great stay."

As the bellman exited, he caught a glimpse of Amy's backside, locked eyes with - and looked away from - a not too happy John. John waited for the door latch to click before turning to Amy.

John said, "Is everything okay?"

"It's beautiful…"

"It has separate rooms. I just thought that this setup would be more convenient for us if we wanted to go over the Kid Crew material later tonight."

"Yeah, John, I'm…not sure…"

He politely ignored her statement and stepped to the windows of the suite. He gazed down on Michigan Avenue and the lake in the near distance.

As he looked to the right he could see the late afternoon sun glistening off of the highly polished, silver, "bean" sculpture in Millennium Park. He smiled at the sight of children running all around it, checking their reflections in the surface of the piece and mugging for their parents' cameras.

"You should see this," he said.

After she didn't make a move to the window, he added, "I wasn't being presumptuous. You're taking the master suite, that's what I had planned."

She didn't believe him, but she smiled and nodded. As she stepped to the window her breath was taken away, partially from her fear of heights, but mostly from the spectacular view.

She said, "It's beautiful, isn't it?"

"Everything looks good from this angle," he said. He took a couple of deep breaths and continued, "If you think I'm coming on too strong, I'm sorry. I really did think that this suite would work for us."

"I'm still trying to get my footing."

"Sure, I get it."

"There's so much that I have to figure out before I get serious with anyone."

"Can I ask you one question?"

"I guess," she said.

"Is there even a chance?"

Her hesitation said it all. He smirked and spun on his heels, heading back toward the middle of the room.

"John…"

"Hey, I almost forgot. I've got to pick something up. I'll be right back," he said nonchalantly as he picked up his overnight bag and walked it into the guest room.

When he emerged a few moments later he wore a blue windbreaker with something bulging out underneath it.

"Go ahead and put your stuff in the master bedroom, relax, and I'll be right back," he said.

Before she could even answer, John walked from the suite.

***

"This is all I need," said the baby face mask-wearing John as he slid $3,500 in neatly bundled $20 bills back across the counter to the terrified, female bank teller.

He stuffed the remaining $10,000 into a white, plastic grocery bag and walked from the bank.

He was pleased with himself by the results in this past week of pretending, twice to date, of being armed; first, at Keith Michaels' house in Inverness, and now, here at this State Street bank branch.

If he was being honest with himself, he'd have to admit that he liked knowing that he would be the only one hurt if things went down the toilet during the commission of one of his crimes.

John exited and turned right on the sidewalk, pulling the mask partially up on his face. As he neared the alleyway next to the building, someone stepped in front of him blocking his path.

It was Amy, and she looked both stricken and terrified.

"What…are you doing?" she whispered.

"Get on the fucking ground!"

Out of his peripheral vision to his left, John could see a uniformed cop crouching and aiming his gun from across State Street.

John shoved past Amy and sprinted as best he could down the alley. The young, Chicago Police officer was almost a half block away when he shouted his demand, so John had just the hint of a lead.

As he hobbled and jogged down the alley, he turned back and could see the Chicago Police officer tug Amy from the opening of the alley and safely around the corner of the building. The Chicago Police officer poked his head back around the corner, but John was gone. He spoke into his shoulder-mounted radio, "I lost him in the alley to the south of the building."

There was an intersecting, northbound alley coming up on

the right. John made the turn and up ahead he could see the heavy, westbound vehicle traffic on the one-way Randolph Street.

He had worked this all out in advance while sitting in the conference room of the Kid Crew offices. From there, he had a vantage point a hundred feet above and could see everything he needed to know to correctly pull this job off.

His plan was to use the maze of one-way streets in the Loop to his advantage. He would be on foot and heading against the flow of traffic, hoping that it would confound the police who'd be arriving in vehicles. With his numb feet and legs, and searing back and hip pain, he needed every advantage he could get.

As he neared Randolph, he peeled off the windbreaker but held onto it. He reached into the white, plastic grocery bag and pulled out a blue-colored, plastic bag and transferred the money from the white to the blue one. He tossed the baby face mask and white bag into a dumpster as he stepped past and made an eastbound turn onto the Randolph Street sidewalk.

Ahead he could see several police cars speeding southbound on State Street.

John crossed over Randolph in the middle of the block and continued heading east toward Michigan Avenue.

The traffic light in front of him turned red. As he waited for the "walk" sign to illuminate at the corner of State and Randolph, John noticed a shabbily-dressed, homeless man asking for change.

John approached him and handed him the windbreaker and said, "I'll give you $20 if you put that on right now."

"Fuck off…"

"I'm serious."

"You some weird fuck who gets off on this shit?"

"I want to help you. That's all," said John.

The homeless man studied John for just a moment, then looked south to where the police activity was escalating. When John didn't want to follow his gaze, he peered back at John with a knowing smirk and said, "$200."

With no time to haggle, John grabbed the money from the blue bag and handed it to the homeless man who quickly flung the coat on.

The light changed and John continued east on Randolph Street. The windbreaker-wearing homeless man immediately quickstepped it northbound on State Street, giggling.

John looked south on State Street and could see five or six Chicago police cars parked willy-nilly at all angles directly in front of the bank. Amy was being questioned, along with a few other bystanders. But what John saw across from the bank stopped him cold in his tracks.

Henry was being held back by a Chicago cop as he stood in the front of another crowd of spectators across the street. He appeared very agitated and raked his hands through his hair as he implored for the Chicago cop to allow him across the street to give Amy some comfort and aid.

Amy, on the other hand, wasn't even paying attention to the questions being thrown at her by yet another cop. She had her eyes on Henry.

Finally, when a suit-wearing bull of a detective confronted Amy, she actually appeared to be responding to the officer's questions. But she happened to peer in John's direction and froze when she caught a glimpse of him. When the detective tried to follow her line of sight, John kept walking.

John had to make it back to the hotel so he could regroup and figure out a way to explain this all to Amy. Or to await his inevitable arrest after Amy told the police who he was and where he was staying.

Now out of the mask, the windbreaker and carrying a different-colored bag, John attempted to stroll as leisurely as he could back to his Michigan Avenue hotel room to await his fate.

"Hey, you! Stop!"

John spun to see the same, young, Chicago Police officer who had initially confronted him outside the bank. The officer was now cautiously edging his way toward John with his police issue Glock .40 in his hand. He wasn't pointing the gun, but he was ready to use it if he had to.

"What's in the bag?"

"Oh, hey, officer, I was at the Best Buy." The smiling and cordial John took a few steps toward the officer as he held the bag open, but the cop was still 50 feet away and couldn't see inside.

"Got a new iTouch. I have the receipt. Is there a problem?" The cop waved John off and turned to continue his search. John wasted no time in hobbling back to his hotel.

CHAPTER
- 41 -

Jimmy was pissed off. So angry he could scream.

He had to hold it together until this Paladin detective, Shane Thompson, got out of his fucking face to unload his frustrations, though.

It had started out as any other quiet, second shift day on the job. A few vandalism reports involving knocked over garbage cans and a lost dog to locate. Not a problem.

As it turned out, the vandalism reports were related to the missing (hungry) dog. When he found the errant pooch, it was in the process of toppling yet another can on Grove Avenue. After he grabbed up the dog and put him in the back seat of the police squad car, the dog let go with the digested remnants of its garbage-collecting ways. So the day soon turned to shit – and it was getting shittier and shittier by the moment.

Now as he sat at his police department desk attempting to eat his 6 p.m. "lunch break" meal of peanut butter and ham on dark rye bread, the square-jawed Detective Thompson had totally fucked up his entire day.

"So you are familiar with the subject?"

"He's not a subject, he's my younger brother," said Jimmy.

"Yeah, right…that's what I had heard."

"What did he do?"

"Do you have a close relationship with your brother?"

That was it, Jimmy had had enough. He stood and took a deep, cleansing breath.

"Listen, Thompson, right?"

"Yeah."

"Fuck off, okay. Either tell me what's going on as a professional courtesy or get the fuck out of my face."

"Why the anger, Officer Caul?"

"Please, call me Jimmy."

The chief poked his head from his office and said, "Everything okay, Flunky- Ah, Caul?"

"This asshole thinks-," but he couldn't go on.

"What? What's going on, Jimmy?" continued the chief.

"This is bullshit…," Jimmy said as he motioned for the chief to mind his own business.

Even the chief was leery of Jimmy when he was in a mood. The other cops in Balmoral were aware of his military past and the stories of the men he single handedly obliterated on that Panamanian beach so many years ago.

Sure, everyone on the force would tease Caul from time to time, but when he sported a face carved in anger, like he was doing now, the smarter co-workers let him be. The chief gave Jimmy and Thompson a polite little wave and ducked back into his office.

Jimmy lost his appetite, and as he moved to toss the remainder of his lunch into a garbage can near the doorway, he continued with, "I've got rounds to make."

"Hold up," said Thompson.

"Yeah?"

Jimmy crossed his arms and awaited the Paladin Detective's next move.

"Just answer me this, okay? Do you think your brother's

capable of doing something like armed robbery?"

"Anyone and everyone is capable of that."

"Have you heard of the Baby Face Robber?"

Jimmy stared for a moment at the Paladin Detective before howling with laughter - more from the sudden need to release some steam - but it was a convincing enough tactic that Thompson smiled.

"Okay, Caul, sorry to put all this shit on you. If you hear anything, though, give me a shout," said Thompson as he placed his business card on Jimmy's desk.

"Who put you on my brother?"

Shane Thompson shrugged, grinned and made his way out of the police department offices.

Jimmy watched him leave before stepping back over to his desk and sliding Thompson's business card into his palm. He crumpled it up and was just about to throw it across the room, when he stopped himself.

CHAPTER
- 42 -

Tyler had taken to openly following Enright.

He didn't trust the sleazebag ex-cop, especially after he pulled that shit with his mom back at the cheap motel. He figured out what was going on, even if his uncle Lou had lied and said nothing had happened between his mother and Enright.

He was now on a mission to shut him down. He could care less if Enright knew he was tailing him because Tyler wasn't afraid of him. He outweighed Enright by at least 60 pounds of solid muscle. If they had to throw down, Tyler would do what he'd have to do and worry about the consequences later.

He figured a nice, tight and crushing bear hug would probably do the trick with the least amount of external blood loss and mess.

What he didn't count on, as he stepped nearer to him, was having Enright kneel and quickly pull a tiny Beretta .380 pistol from the ankle holster strapped to his pasty leg.

The older man had shoved the gun under the surprised Tyler's chin and leaned in close to the kid's face. This happened when Tyler's anger had boiled over, and he called out Enright in a parking lot near the Balmoral train station.

Enright did size up the kid and knew that his Krav Maga skills could do some damage to the muscular teen, but he would probably work up a sweat in the process. And his stomach was a little upset from the Gyro sandwich he had earlier at Dink's Diner, so the gun would do the trick this time.

"Okay, kid, now what? It's your move…"

"Fuck you. Pull the trigger," said Tyler.

Enright lowered the gun and took a step back. He gave Tyler a look of admiration.

"You're stopping today. You no longer work for me. And you leave my mom alone."

"Yeah, yeah, and if I don't you'll kill me or some bullshit, right?"

"That's right. If my dad finds out about what you pulled with me and my mom, I'll do it myself. You can't let him find out about any of this. Just drop it. Keep the $4,500. I don't give a shit about that. Fuck you if you think I'm paying you that extra ten grand, though. Especially after the shit you've pulled."

Tyler was an intelligent kid but obviously not very worldly. Enright could tell the moment they met at the ice cream and donut place. He could plainly see that the young man had always enjoyed a cushy, suburban existence. It just oozed from his pores.

Enright knew, shit, anyone could discern immediately, that Tyler could do some serious damage if allowed to take it to that physical level. He was huge. But he had a blind spot when it came to his family's honor.

Anyone else would have easily seen that Enright was never going to stop fucking with them and their loved ones, but Tyler, Tyler seemed to actually believe him when he said, "I'm done messing with you, kid. I don't need you anymore. I did what you paid me to do, and I found the guy. You do what you want from this point on. I'll go my way, okay? I'll leave your family be."

Tyler was skeptical but seemed to be buying what Enright was selling. He said, "Just leave 'em alone…"

As the kid stepped back to his Jeep Cherokee, Enright smiled to himself and thought, "What an asshole. I'm going to up the ask from Tyler's pop to $100,000 now. Stupid fucker. Hell, I may even get that piece of ass from his fine mom, too."

CHAPTER
- 43 -

The vibe in the conference room for the second day of Kid Crew instruction was, for the lack of a better word, weird.

John tried to plead with his eyes for her to just acknowledge him. Henry paid extra special and, frankly, annoying attention to the crime victim/witness, Amy. Henry carried on as if she was an expectant mother more than a student, constantly asking if she was comfortable, getting her water, etc. John thought it nauseating.

Amy was completely pissed off at John, but she had a lot on her mind and a ton of calculating to do. Yes, she was extremely angry for having been vaulted into his robbery scheme, even if it was on the periphery of the crime.

He was the goddamned Baby Face Robber from the news. But she couldn't help but admire John's wile and guts when he robbed and got away cleanly from the downtown Chicago bank. The very same bank she was looking at now from the windows in the Kid Crew conference room. It was quite obvious that she hadn't turned John in for committing the crime the day before.

And it was also clear that she was still on board for managing the Kid Crew. She really needed this to happen, and for the moment, that outweighed any sniggling thought of having John arrested.

He was the Baby Face Robber. God, he was the perfect person to pull off such a scheme, she thought. He was handsome, a little unassuming, and friendly, too. Without the mask on or armed with a pistol, no one would ever suspect him. But she also hadn't lived in Balmoral her entire life. The townspeople there would utter his name without hesitation if asked if he was capable of such a thing. Mr. James at the BMW dealership was proof of that.

He had awaited his fate for two hours in that lovely and lonely hotel suite on Michigan Avenue the night before.

He purposefully wore a simple, tight, white t-shirt and jeans so when the police did storm the room, they'd see instantly that he wasn't hiding any weapons.

He took chances during his robberies, but he didn't have a death wish. His overnight bag was packed and sitting by the door of the suite, and the door itself was propped open by the secondary, flip-locking system. This would allow the police easy access.

And when the door did finally push open, John closed his eyes and raised his hands, awaiting his imminent arrest. The clinking and clanging of rolling carts and the friendly voices of Amy, the chef and his assistant, made him open an eye. He stood there and blinked a lot, lowered his arms, smiled and said, "Hey, dinner's here. Great."

After the chef and his cooking partner had left, John and Amy, sat on opposite love seats with a coffee table between them, and dug hungrily into their meals. It was if they hadn't eaten in days.

After the meal of sautéed, French-style, lemon chicken and miniature, red bistro potatoes braised in chicken stock and fresh asparagus, Amy finally broke her silence.

"I don't want to talk about it. Ever," she said.

John smiled, knowing he was going to be able to keep his scheme going for a little while longer. Maybe Amy wasn't as romantically interested in him as he was in her, but he still wanted to get the Kid Crew franchise up and running. He was actually excited about being a business owner. Maybe if she cooled off for a few days, John could put romantic feelers out there again. But he was free to move forward now and possibly save the Fourth of July Festival and embarrass his hometown as well.

Amy seemed relaxed but didn't like the self-satisfied look on John's face one little bit.

"And go fuck yourself for getting me into this," she said, as she picked up a small plate of cheesecake from the coffee table and dug in with her fork.

CHAPTER
- 44 -

The train ride home from downtown Chicago was, not surprisingly, a silent one.

Gone were John's inane and excitedly spoken bits of trivia about the areas they passed through. Also erased was Amy's faux interest in what John was pointing out.

At the Balmoral stop, Amy walked her way through the darkened parking lot and hailed a cab for the ride back to her friend Lori's house in Lake Zurich. John began hoofing it the four blocks to his house on Coleridge.

Actually there was one awkward and quick conversation as the doors to the train opened, and Amy began walking away from John. She had turned and said, "Start getting the store put together. We need to get this thing launched as soon as possible - and you're doubling my salary."

That was just fine with John.

On his walk home, he couldn't help but smile at the thought of seeing the beautiful Amy every day at the Kid Crew franchise. This was going to all work out after all.

"What the fuck are you doing with my mom, dude?"

John stopped in his tracks. He couldn't see Danny just yet, but he knew he was in the bushes to the side of the massive home he now stood in front of. When he emerged, the young man was shaking with anger and looked like he was ready to fight.

"I saw the two of you. I saw it, man, in that parking lot. When she got home she was in her bedroom and crying. What did you do?"

"Nothing. I didn't do anything, Danny. You have to believe me."

John did the right thing by turning down Danny's mom, Sharon, in the parking lot of the soon-to-be Kid Crew franchise. He didn't want to go into specific details about the brief meeting that Danny must've witnessed from a distance.

"Danny, there's no problem. Nothing is going on, okay?"

But Danny didn't believe him – evident by the wayward punch he launched at John's head. John ducked under Danny's swinging fist and grabbed him in a tight hug.

"Danny, please. Nothing happened."

Danny violently wriggled himself free and spun on John, pointing his finger in his face.

"We do the robbery in the next few days or I talk."

He ran away, leaving John to stand there holding his overnight bag and pondering how most of his not-so-well-thought-out plans had gone to shit.

CHAPTER
- 45 -

"Well, here's the thing. I need this to look like maybe a jewelry store or something before making it into the Kid Crew."

Sitting in the living room of the tiny house on Coleridge, Larry and Dwayne were instantly confused.

Dwayne said, "A jewelry store? I don't get it."

John knew they were thrown off by his remark, but he couldn't let on just yet that he was going to use the space to fake a robbery with Danny. The way John saw it, Danny would not be the wiser, and he'd keep his promise of pulling off a Baby Face Robber job to get him off his back.

Dwayne said, "Why a jewelry store?"

John said, "Or just something other than the Kid Crew..."

Larry and Dwayne shared a confused glance before Larry turned his attention to the pacing John.

"Is everything okay, John?"

"Yeah. No. Yeah, it's fine."

"Why not make it look like a lumber clearance center since you'll have all the wood for the Kid Crew build-out lying around and piled everywhere."

"Genius, Larry. That's perfect!" said John. "We'll use the front counter that's already there. I'll need a cash register, too."

The sudden, loud opening and slamming of the back door startled all of them.

"John? Where the fuck are you?" screamed Jimmy from the kitchen.

John hurried into the kitchen and was instantly grabbed by the angry Jimmy. "Paladin PD is onto you! You stupid son of a bitch!"

"Jimmy, I've got people-"

"I'm not going down with you."

"There's people in the other-"

"I'll testify against you, brother. I have no problem doing that. You will not fuck me and my family over, do you understand me? I told you that this Baby Face Robber bullshit is insane!"

Jimmy finally lost a bit of rage when he heard Larry clear his throat in the living room. He pushed John away and charged into the front room where he found Larry and Dwayne both smiling and sitting politely.

"Hey, officer," said Dwayne, pointing to the coffee table, "There's Bundt cake if you're interested. Lemon curd."

"Hello," countered Larry with a wan smile.

"Oh, fuck me! John! Goddamn it!!"

John gently placed a hand on Jimmy's shoulder, and his brother didn't shrug it away. He looked more and more like he needed a hug.

Dwayne stood and approached Jimmy, and said, "First of all, Jimmy, we won't tell anyone anything, right, Larry?"

Larry was still smiling and nodding. He had a new and even stronger appreciation for the outcast John. "Poking the man in the eye? I love it!" he said. "How long have you-"

"Please, stop. Stop talking about it. Shit, what are we going to do?" said Jimmy.

Dwayne, without hesitation, said, "Nothing. We don't do or say shit."

Everyone looked at him so he finished out his thought. "We let it be. No one will know, Jimmy."

Jimmy plopped onto the couch and said, "But I had a Paladin PD detective question me about John today. Someone is definitely onto him."

Dwayne sat next to Jimmy and said, "Are they gonna arrest him? No. They'd a done did it by now. What proof do they have? None, I'm guessing, otherwise old John would be in the pen by now. Right?"

But Jimmy and John knew otherwise. Jimmy said, "What about Lou, and his brother…and his son?"

Larry chimed in, "Lou knows? Shit…"

Dwayne laughed and said, "That's why he's giving John free food."

Both Jimmy and John nodded grimly. Before John added, "Jimmy, they won't talk. It'll blow up in their faces if they do. They don't want that kid to lose out on a football scholarship and all that. There's no way."

CHAPTER
- 46 -

John stood on State Street peering into the bank branch he had robbed. The very same teller he had gotten the money from a few days prior, playfully spoke with the male customer she assisted.

The terror John had seen in her eyes was gone today and that warmed his heart. He was so conflicted about his robbing activities. The urge to start up the Kid Crew and finance the Fourth of July Festival, which was quickly approaching, was strong, but the feeling of guilt and shame was building to a very close second.

After strolling from the area of the bank, John made his way to the law offices on East Haddock Place near Harold Washington College. There he stepped into the lobby of a nearly 100-year-old building, entered the antiquated elevator and punched the button for the ninth floor. Arriving in the tiny alcove that was the ninth floor, he took the three steps toward the law office door.

He had set up this meeting with his father's friend, George, the man responsible for John's childhood white-knuckle boat rides on Lake Geneva. It was time to start making things more than right. He owed that much to a lot of people whose lives he had inappropriately affected in the past weeks.

CHAPTER
- 47 -

To John's specifications, Larry had put the finishing touches on a series of roosters and apples he painted on the back wall of the former carpet company and soon-to-be Kid Crew franchise. Larry was a master with the spray paint can, never allowing the dried paint to clog the spray tip, thus giving his work a crisp, textured and surreal look.

The roosters and apples he created were not of the same ilk as the ones in John's kitchen. They were more colorful, playful - whimsical, even. Something a small child would enjoy viewing day in and day out. Absolutely nothing like the tit-fucking Godzilla he had painted on that yuppie couple's garage in Bucktown.

Larry was growing as an artist and he was proud of his work.

Dwayne was busy erecting piles of raw materials to make it look like this was a lumber wholesaler of sorts. They'd start the real build-out of the Kid Crew in a day or two, but for now, staging was the name of the game.

John had to shake Danny from tailing him that morning. The kid had seen the structure where the Kid Crew would soon be located because it was in the parking lot where John had disrespected Danny's mother. But the kid didn't know that John had leased the building.

So when he spotted Danny following him at breakfast time, John had done most of what Enright did to get the drop on Rita. He snuck out the side door at Dink's Diner and worked his way around the back side of the business where Danny couldn't see from his vantage point at the Superstar's Coffee Shop across the street.

John had gotten away cleanly and now, as he plugged in and tested the old cash register he'd borrowed from Lou's basement at Dink's Diner, the door opened and in walked Henry.

John was so surprised to see him all the way out here in Balmoral that he didn't even recognize him for a full two seconds.

"Wow. It's looking great," said Henry, even though it really didn't.

John surveyed the space – the wood being piled here and there, the crappy carpeting that needed to be pulled up, the shitty front counter that was on its last legs and the dropped ceiling tiles looking as if they would cave in at any moment, and instantly thought, "Oh, shit, what's he want now?"

"Is everything okay, Henry?"

"Couldn't be better," Henry lied. "Um, can we talk?"

"Okay."

Henry turned and pushed his way out the door and into the parking lot. John stepped outside in time to see Henry moving around the back of the building.

John let out a slow breath knowing that this wasn't going to be a pleasant conversation. He followed Henry to where the dumpster was located out of view of busy Route 14.

"What is it, Henry?"

"Place is looking fantastic. I know this is going to be a super successful location-"

"What's going on?"

"I need $100,000. If I don't get it, I'm finished. We are

finished."

"What about the $10,000 I just gave you? I thought that was to get that new guy started on selling more franchises."

"Yeah, well…I read his email incorrectly. I missed seeing a zero. It was an honest mistake."

"Bullshit. What are you doing to me?"

"Okay, all right. I'm sorry, John. I thought I could talk him down to starting with a $10,000 bonus and not the entire 100 grand that he said he needed. But he balked, okay?"

"What if I just walk away and cut my losses? What would happen then?"

"No Kid Crew franchise, no Amy," said Henry.

Henry knew exactly why John was really interested in the franchise to begin with. He could tell the moment he met both Amy and John at the convention center that John wasn't truly interested in the business, but more in the beautiful Amy.

Henry added, "But I have to be honest, man. I just don't see you two as a couple. She's more, I don't know, my speed."

"Is that right?"

"Hey, just being honest."

"Right. You're all about the honesty," said John.

"I love her, John. I love Amy."

"Christ."

"I can't lose this company and the chance to be with her." Henry's eyes actually brimmed with tears. It threw John off his anger for just a moment.

"Get out of here."

"I need that money, John. I have to have it. If I can't have Amy, I can still have my business."

"Go, Henry. Leave me alone."

"I think the Chicago police would be interested to know that you like wearing baby face masks and popping into banks, don't you? Especially banks that are right across the street from my office where I make it a habit of watching passersby coming and going when I'm not working. It relaxes me. Usually."

"You…asshole…"

"I'm a desperate man, John. You're right that this isn't how I'd normally operate. But I really need this all to work out for me. I hope you can see it my way."

"Hey, there you are," said Dwayne, startling both John and Henry. "Sorry, guys. John do you have a pry bar? I need to separate some of this stuff and the hammer's not cuttin' it."

"No, sorry. Wait. I do at the house," said John as he dug a hand into his pants pocket coming back out with the car keys to his old station wagon. He tossed the keys to Dwayne and said, "In the garage. It'll be hanging on the wall near the freezer."

Dwayne jingled the keys, nodded and was gone.

"Please think about it, John. I'm sorry that it had to come to this. Please believe me. I really do need the money for the business. I'm not making that up. I'll need an answer tonight."

John watched as Henry headed back to where his car was parked in front of the building. He dropped his head and considered how he had gotten himself into the many jams he had of late.

The bottom line for John was that he knew he had no one to blame but himself.

***

Enright loudly yanked up the floorboards in John's bedroom closet, with the very same pry bar Dwayne was on the way over to pick up.

His hands were busy doing the work but his mind was racing as he thought about the attractive, blonde woman who had winked at him while he was getting a cup of coffee at Superstar's Coffee just an hour or so before.

She had that curvy build that Enright always looked for in a woman. He usually paid for such women to jump into the sack with him, so having a possible freebie coming down the pike would be a new experience for him.

After getting his coffee he had turned and noticed that

the blonde was gone. He wasn't completely deflated, though. Balmoral was a small town. He'd see her again, he thought.

Enright had no idea that the old station wagon was pulling up the driveway. He had been in the house for over an hour tearing it up piece by piece looking for any evidence of the robberies.

And maybe evidence was too general of a term, really. Enright was looking for the money. He just wasn't aware that, basically, the money was in the possession of a guy named Franky "Five Bucks" after Keith Michaels had paid him back his investment funds in the failed land deal.

As he pulled into John's driveway, Dwayne noticed the nondescript car parked two doors down. The driver and the passenger looked a lot like Lou and his brother Jason, but both wore plain, black baseball caps and black t-shirts. Through the glare off the windshield, Dwayne couldn't really get a good look at them anyway. The two men, in unison, had dropped their gaze, covering their faces with the bills of their hats.

Dwayne stopped the car just outside the garage. He didn't know it yet, but Tyler, driving his maroon Jeep, had just parked on Monument Street at the rear of John's house.

He had been following Enright and knew he was inside John's house and that John was away. Enright may or may not have noticed Tyler tailing him, but the soon-to-be defensive end for Boston College could give a rat's ass.

He had lied to Enright back at the train station. He was finally going to take care of Enright once and for all.

Tyler quickly got out of his car carrying something long and slender and rolled up in a sleeping bag. Tyler made his way through the side yard of the home on Monument and angled toward John's house.

In the rental car parked a few houses from John's home, Jason and Lou made sure that their weapons were ready to go.

Both were wearing plastic disposable gloves. Lou was armed with a leather sap and Jason with a piano wire garrote. They'd done this type of wet work in the distance past, when they both had lived in Greece, but neither of them had actually had to kill someone before.

They were a bit rusty, but killing was more a mental skill than a physical one, they figured. If you had your head compartmentalized in such a way that the blood, begging and screaming didn't bother you too much, the physical part was a piece of cake.

Lou didn't want to tell Jason about this Enright character, but the thought that he was keeping something important from the one who trusted him the most ate away at his conscience.

Lou finally broke down and told Jason all about what Tyler and Rita had gotten themselves into. And now they were ready to fix this family problem once and for all.

***

Larry had left for the day, and Dwayne still hadn't arrived back with his car, so John locked up the building and began walking home. The car horn startled him as he approached the railroad tracks.

Amy, behind the wheel of her old car, waved for John to get in, which he quickly did. They glanced at one another but looked away almost immediately. They drove in silence for a few blocks.

"Thanks. Dwayne has my car."

"Oh"

"John, I know I said we should never talk about what happened, but I think we should now. What's going to happen?"

"Nothing. Nothing ever happens."

She took a right on Main instead of going straight to John's street, and when John didn't offer any more information, she continued, "No, really. What's going to happen, John? I mean, you can't do something like that and not expect to get away with it."

"Where are you going? I live the other way."

As Amy pulled into the high school parking lot to turn around, she stopped and took in the sight of the construction crews repairing the crumbling, gymnasium foundation.

They had created a complex system of footers and piers to bolster the sizeable building while a new foundation was poured underneath the damaged one.

"So, you and Henry, huh?"

"What?"

"You don't have to pretend, Amy, I know that you guys are into one another."

"I really don't know what you're talking about. And you know what? I don't like your tone."

"So you didn't put him up to it?"

"What are you talking about!?"

Her outburst cemented everything in John's mind – she actually didn't know about Henry's love for her or that he was shaking him down for an additional $100,000 to prop up his failing, Kid Crew business. He had to know for certain, though, and provoking her was the fastest way to finding out.

John let the air settle and watched the construction crew along with Amy, neither of them wanting to make eye contact with the other.

"It wasn't an accident, you know," said John.

"What are you talking-"

But she actually did know what John was referring to. She had discovered his possible arsonist past and nickname of Sparky after she began asking around town about John.

"I figured that the cotton from the stage clouds I was making would go up like a shot if I crammed enough of it into the powered-up light housings. I plugged it in and pushed the entire lighting system under the first row of bleachers. Man, it was something. I barely got out of the gym myself before it became totally engulfed."

"John, please stop talking. I don't want to know any more, okay?"

John sat silently for a moment and truly admired what the construction crew had accomplished in just a few days. They had to work quickly, though, if they were going to save the gymnasium's structure.

John said, "Go to dinner with me tomorrow night?"

"And why would I want to do that?! So we can go out after and knock over a liquor store."

"Meet me at the Bistro on Route 14 at eight. You know where it is."

"Or, what?" asked Amy.

John just smiled and shrugged his shoulders. He seemed to be sporting a more "dick-ish" side of his personality.

"Oh, I get it. Go to dinner with me and back to my house afterwards or there's no Kid Crew job, is that it? I knew it. I knew it would come to this."

"You would look good in an orange jumpsuit."

"You asshole! I had nothing to do with that shit you pulled downtown!"

"I don't know. You did spend the night in a bank robber's hotel suite. You had a nice meal cooked by a private chef, and all. How will that look to a jury?"

"Get out!"

"So I'll see you tomorrow at eight?"

"Out!!"

As John got out of her car Amy took off, almost taking his left foot along for the ride.

All he could think of was, "Shit."

He still had a half mile walk to see what had become of his car and Dwayne. But he stopped for a brief moment to watch the construction crew do their thing and thought, "She'll be there."

***

"Dad? What are you doing?"

Jason, trying to wrap the garrote around Enright's thick neck, was thrown off for just an instant, and that allowed the chubby, private detective to spin and hammer Jason with a series of quick elbow and forearm jabs to the head.

Jason went down hard, blood pouring from his nose and mouth. He lay prone next to the already unconscious and bloody Dwayne and Lou. Both of whom had been quickly dispatched by the very adept, Krav Maga fighter, Enright.

Earlier, Dwayne hadn't even put up a fight. Enright finally heard the car door of the old station wagon shut and thought that John had arrived back home.

Just as Enright had stepped into the kitchen, Dwayne walked into the house. Enright took him down with a quick shot with the heel of his hand to the underside of the unsuspecting man's chin.

Dwayne was a tough guy, fending for himself day in and day out in prison, but he was no match for the maniacal Enright.

As it happened, Lou and Jason barged through the front door as Enright was dragging Dwayne's unconscious body into the living room by a single ankle.

Lou was able to get a strike in with the leather sap, but it was a glancing blow. Enright instantly cold-cocked Lou with a thunderous series of elbow strikes to his head and neck. Lou went down in a heap.

Jason wasn't intimidated by Enright at all. In fact, they traded equal blows – fists, elbows and knee strikes. Jason was finally able to spin to Enright's flank and whip the garrote around his neck.

That's when Tyler pushed his way through the back door with the shotgun still wrapped in the sleeping bag. Seeing his kid there startled Jason, and that's when Enright got the drop on him.

Enright said, "Give me the gun, kid."

Tyler tried in vain to unfurl the sleeping bag from the 12 gauge shotgun, but Enright got to him first. The private detective ripped the gun from Tyler's grasp and spun it around on him.

***

John was exhausted and totally pissed off as he turned the corner from Dundee to Coleridge. The anger wasn't directed at Dwayne for not returning his car, though.

He was irritated for allowing things to get out of hand with Amy. He could only hope that his clearer mind would help to make things right in the coming days.

As he neared his home all he could think about was taking a hot shower and maybe getting a nap.

He was now completely Vicodin-free. His mind was cleaner than it had been in a few years. His newfound sobriety empowered him.

He wanted to now take an even more ambitious approach with his life. A legally ambitious approach, that is. He was a small business owner and very proud of that fact. It took a lot of effort to kick the Vikes. And many more sleepless and nauseated nights to accomplish than he expected, but he did it.

She would be there tomorrow night, he thought. She wouldn't dare not show up. Amy needed the job and she had no other opportunities in her pipeline. She'd be there.

***

When Enright pulled the trigger on the shotgun, nothing happened. He forgot to take the safety off.

"Fuck! Fuck!" screamed Enright.

Tyler didn't hesitate. He pounded on Enright with a series of fast, yet ineffective, punches. It was enough to knock Enright back toward the kitchen table, where he lost his balance, dropped the gun and fell to the floor.

Tyler dove on top of Enright, but the older combatant had the Krav Maga advantage yet again. He violently wriggled to a better fighting position and put Tyler into a triangle choke hold and began applying pressure.

The more the kid fought, the faster he was losing consciousness. Just as the kid went limp, John walked into the back door.

"What the hell-"

Enright got to his feet and hurled himself at John. But John's base instincts kicked in. All those fights fending off the bullies at

Balmoral High would benefit John in this battle.

His frustrations over being the town's outcast all these 20 years bubbled up in John, and he became instantly enraged.

He was actually a near match for Enright's fighting prowess, too. That and Enright had already fought off several combatants. He was fricking tired.

John was a master of the body punch, though, lifting Enright off his feet with every hammering fist he placed into the chubby man's rib cage. What Enright accomplished with elbow hits and knee strikes, John did with old-fashioned, solidly placed punches.

Enright finally got a wider opening and caught John with a well-placed forearm shot to his nose. The score was instantly evened.

John staggered backward, and Enright went right after him.

As Enright rained down blow after blow, John was able to simultaneously deflect some of the hits with his left arm, while he picked up a ceramic rooster teapot from the kitchen counter with his right hand. He smashed the private detective in the ear with the teapot. Bits of ceramic shattered everywhere.

"Tyler! Tyler, are you okay?" the waking Jason said from the living room floor. "Lou! Brother, wake up."

"What the fuck, man," said a groggy Dwayne, attempting to get to his feet.

And that's when the blonde woman from Superstar's Coffee, the one who had winked at Enright, walked right into the house, pushed Dwayne aside and angled toward the kitchen.

"What the hell?" said Dwayne as he plopped down into an overstuffed chair.

In the kitchen Enright had quick-kicked John in the shin but without effect. Enright, his exhaustion level at its max, was surprised that the kick had no effect on John.

John said, "Can't feel my legs, asshole."

Enright noticed the blonde woman first and tried reaching for the shotgun that was lying across the threshold between the kitchen and the living room. But in one fluid motion, and only using one hand, the blonde woman picked it up first, snicked the safety off and placed the shotgun barrel right under Enright's chin.

Enright was too tired to do anything about it, but he didn't raise his hands either.

"Hi, Enright," said Rita, as she peeled off the blonde wig with her free hand.

Enright did one last stupid thing before he took his final breath. He tried slapping the gun away. He hadn't figured on the level of pressure Rita's finger had on the trigger, though.

The thunderous boom finally woke even the unconscious Lou.

Three minutes later, when the two Balmoral police cars arrived in front of the house, John was setting off cherry bombs in the driveway.

"Hey, John, what the hell, man?" said Jimmy, walking closer.

A sheepish John said, "Shit. Sorry, guys. Are you receiving complaints? I'm getting in the Fourth of July mood a little early, I guess. Sorry. Really. I'll stop now."

The other cop was actually the chief. He surveyed John's house, the egg stains and the general crappy condition of the structure. He turned to Jimmy and said, "Take care of this." The chief spun on his heels, walked back to his car, got in and took off.

"What happened?" said Jimmy, pointing to the blood trickling out of John's nose and over his upper lip.

"I cut myself shaving. It must've opened back up," he lied.

Jimmy didn't buy the story but didn't really care one way or the other. As he was about to leave, he noticed Tyler carrying something rather large, heavy and covered in dark, plastic bags into the open garage.

"What the fuck…"

***

Jimmy had his gun out of the holster but wasn't aiming it at any one particular person as of yet.

All but one of the still breathing players stood in a circle in the closed garage. John, Jimmy, Lou, Jason, Rita, and Tyler were all looking rather grim. All but Jimmy and Rita were nursing their wounds with paper towel-covered handfuls of ice.

Jimmy said, "I have to cuff someone. Who's it going to be?"

Dwayne, on the other hand, whistled to himself as he moved stacks of frozen pizza boxes from the large chest freezer in the corner. Enright's dark, plastic bag-covered body lay across the work table next to the freezer.

"Okay, boy, he's all yours," Dwayne said to Tyler. Tyler's eyes asked Jimmy for permission to help Dwayne and that's when the Balmoral cop sighed and put his gun away.

Jimmy nodded for Tyler to go ahead and help. Tyler made his way over and lifted Enright's body and unceremoniously dropped it into the freezer. Dwayne slammed the lid closed and smiled in a self-congratulatory way.

"We're gonna have to eat this shit up," Dwayne said, pointing to the frozen pizzas he had displaced to make room for Enright's corpse. "Those pizzas ain't cheap."

John said, "It's not a problem, really. I got them as two-fers at Gemstone last week-"

"Holy shit, will you shut the fuck up?" said Jimmy. "We've got to think this through."

But John had already done the calculating; he had just not let anyone in on his plan yet. He stepped over to his workbench and grabbed up a brand-new, drum file power tool, unboxed it and said, "Lou, hand me the shotgun."

CHAPTER
- 48 -

After a hearty breakfast of corned beef hash and poached eggs, John and Dwayne parted ways. Larry watched as they shook hands and then "bro hugged" in the parking lot.

Larry knew something was up with John and Dwayne but didn't want to know any more than he already did. John was the damned Baby Face Robber. Shit, he thought, "I know it's wrong, but I'm proud of my friend."

"It's his last day as dishwasher," said a smiling Lou as he stepped up to the kitchen pass-through. "Dwayne's moving on."

"No shit. I didn't know that," said Larry.

"The man is good man. He's good for his word," said Lou as he made his way over to seat an arriving customer.

John made his way back into the diner and poked his head through the pass-through and said, "Larry, are you up for making $500 later on today? It's nothing illegal. For you, anyway." John winked.

Larry smiled and nodded. He'd be honored to help his friend.

***

Dwayne was able to steal the tan-colored Saturn only two

blocks away from Dink's Diner at the train station parking lot.

He thought, "Shit, John was right, Saturn's are easy to hot-wire." He put the car into drive and waved at a female parking enforcement officer who was ticketing a car.

"You have a good day, officer," said Dwayne, as he slowly rolled away in the stolen car.

***

John, carrying a large manila envelope, met a kitchen staff member of the Bistro on Route 14 at the back door of the restaurant. The dinner date with Amy wouldn't be until eight that evening, but John had something that needed setting up beforehand.

The suspicious kitchen staff member didn't want to allow John into the building. That was, until John tucked a crisp, hundred dollar bill in the staff member's white shirt pocket.

When he was given permission to enter, John quickly moved inside.

***

Keith Michaels was handed a large manila envelope by a male assistant as he sat in his village council member office at the municipal building.

After the assistant made his exit, Keith studied the envelope carefully before he ripped it open. It had his name handwritten on the front, but there was not a return address or cancelled postage on it and that made him a little suspicious.

After he ripped it open, the first thing that dropped out of the envelope was a flattened, plastic, baby face mask. When that happened, Keith got immediately to his feet, crossed the room and shut the office door.

When he stepped back over to his desk, he emptied the remainder of the envelope's contents out onto his desk. A handwritten note and two separate cashier's checks lay on the desk top. Keith picked up the note and read it, smiled and looked at one of the checks.

"Holy shit!"

Keith's confidence of late was skyrocketing, and he had no one else to thank but the man in the baby face mask. He's the one who had helped make it possible for Keith to replenish his own savings account, and to finally pay off Franky "Five Bucks" of the $50,000 he owed - and to get out from under his mobbed-up thumb.

But there was more to Keith's rising confidence level than ridding himself of Franky's wrath.

Keith Michaels had finally stood up to his overbearing father-in-law.

After being allowed to get off the financial hook he was on, Keith had moved his family out of the million dollar home in Inverness. He had relocated back into the fixer-upper he was working on in Balmoral. He left the house keys as well as the keys for the leased car in the parked Mercedes SUV in the driveway of the Inverness home.

And something rather special happened during this new course of events in Keith's life – his wife and family seemed to be responding quite positively to the new Keith.

It wasn't that he had become overbearing himself, but that he was more attentive and caring. He was now spending much more time with his family instead of chasing his wayward dreams and trying to satisfy a father-in-law who would never be pleased anyway.

Keith's wife was happy to go along with dumping the big house for the one that was more centrally located in the cute little town of Balmoral. There her family, especially her disabled son, could thrive and be more connected to the community, instead of hiding in a cul-de-sac in Inverness.

The day they moved into the old house in Balmoral, Franky "Five Bucks" called again. This time he wanted Keith to pay the additional $100,000 promised in their initial deal.

Franky didn't even feign any pleasantries this time around. But Keith had grown a spine, though - something that Franky didn't expect.

"Frederick, do you really want to go down this road? Hey, I'm talking to you, Frederick Gregers of 12 East Arthur Avenue in Oak Park?"

"How do you know this?" said the supremely surprised Franky "Five Bucks" in his Chicago/Danish accent.

"I've been watching you, Frederick. You may want to change up your routine. You do the same thing every day. You go to the same places. You're very predictable," said Keith.

It was true, too. Franky "Five Bucks" hated changing up his normal, daily activities and routine. He was very set in his ways.

He woke at six, showered, dressed and went to breakfast at the same greasy diner every day of the week. He would do some phone work from the front room of his house and then head back to the same diner for lunch at 11:45. By one in the afternoon, he was back on the phone at his house, mostly collecting on debts owed to him.

Business was good, too. At 4:45, Franky would head right back to the exact same diner. And by six in the evening, he settled back in at home for a night of DVR'd game shows and America's Funniest Home Videos reruns. Day in and day out, it was always the same for Franky "Five Bucks."

"You fuck! You don't threaten me!"

"Frederick, you're not used to dealing with guys like me. I'm willing to put it all on the line," Keith lied. "I'll take you out, and I don't care if I die doing it. In fact, that's exactly what I want. That way my family will get the life insurance. I want to die, Frederick. Want to join me?"

There was a long silence on the phone line. "You leave me alone," said a shaky Franky "Five bucks," and he hung up.

And it really wouldn't matter if Keith had actually followed through on his threat or not because within six months Frederick - Franky "Five Bucks" - Gregers would be dead from a massive heart attack – brought on by stress and his lousy eating habits.

Keith sat back down at his desk, picked up the phone and

dialed. "Have the finance director come to my office immediately. The Fourth of July Festival will be on after all. What? Right now, yes. And who's in charge of making new signs? Okay, put me through to him."

With the phone cradled between his ear and shoulder, he spun in his chair and put the note and the envelope through his shredder – but he kept the baby face mask as a souvenir.

***

Gretchen, the shampoo tech from the spa in Deer Park, left work early after receiving a similar envelope as the one Keith had just opened in his office.

Now, as she stood in the teller line at her bank, propped up on crutches, and sporting a new knee brace, she wondered if she would even go back to her minimum wage spa job ever again.

Maybe she would finally look into attending college. Or she could travel. That was something she always dreamed about when she was growing up back in Iowa. Who wouldn't want to trade an ocean of corn rows to having Jamaican cornrows placed in their hair while gazing at the real ocean?

She did make up her mind about one thing, though, when she was the next customer to be helped by the teller, a handsome man about her age. She definitely wouldn't even bother going back to the spa again. The $100,000 cashier's check in her hand would see her through for a while, she was quite sure of that.

The handwritten note that was placed into the large envelope along with the check apologized for the injury she received when she aggravated her knee chasing down John. "I'm glad that I didn't tackle that asshole…" said Gretchen to herself.

"What was that?" asked the handsome teller.

Gretchen smiled and waved her own comment away as she hobbled forward to deposit her check.

"Hey, what are you doing after work?" she asked the teller with a self-assured smirk on her face.

***

The very same hotel clerk that John had robbed at gunpoint in the upscale, Lake Geneva hotel couldn't believe his bad luck.

This would be twice that he was robbed by the asshole wearing a baby face mask. The poor guy was still battling the emotional turmoil that the last robbery brought to his life.

He tried to cover for it when he was at work, but he was terrified most days. He had spent many sleepless nights seeing the robbery play out as if on a video loop. He needed to regain the carefree life he had led up to the point of being robbed.

To do that the hotel clerk needed empowerment in his life, and fast. The psychologist he had been seeing ever since the crime occurred had also advised him of the same thing. If he could get control over smaller portions of his life, things would return to normal for him.

But something was different this time around. The Baby Face Robber didn't point a gun at him. He actually slid a pile of bundled bills back across the counter as if making a deposit at a bank.

The hotel clerk made his move. He dove over the counter, tackled the assailant and pinned his arms behind his back. He didn't really know what came over him, but he knew he had to act, and act quickly. He was pissed that this baby face mask-wearing asshole had ruined his life.

"Okay, man, take her easy. Brother, I'm giving the money back, can't you see?" said Dwayne under the baby face mask.

"Call the cops," screamed the hotel clerk.

"Don't bother, brother, I already called 'em," said Dwayne. "Hey, you know anything about the chow in the prisons here? I heard it's pretty good. You wouldn't mind taking this mask off my face, would ya? Kinda stuffy."

***

John strolled along the streets of his Balmoral neighborhood with a plastic grocery bag full of loose, fresh eggs.

He was eyeing potential targets.

He stopped in front of the house that was owned by Emil, the 80-year-old Dink's Diner regular. Emil was most likely responsible for a few of the egg stains back at John's home. Maybe more than a few of the stains, but John didn't have definitive proof.

By the way Emil had treated him for the past 20 years, yelling from afar that he had ruined his son's life, he was pretty sure he was an egg tosser.

John reached into the bag and gently grasped a single egg. He hefted the small sphere, gauging its weight and how much power he would need to launch it, directly into the large, picture window at the front of the home.

John was surprised when Emil himself stepped into the living room of his home and peered out at him.

Emil noticed John, the egg and John's smirk. He flipped John the bird.

But John didn't throw the egg. He had a change of plan. He simply walked up the driveway of Emil's house and toward his garage.

"You better not, Sparky!" said Emil, standing at an open window in his kitchen, as John stepped inside the garage. "Hey, what in the hell are you doing?"

John dragged one of Emil's empty garbage cans out of the garage and placed it in the middle of the driveway, just as Emil charged from his back door.

"I'm calling your brother. He'll arrest you for trespassing."

"I have a good feeling that he won't," said John.

"Screw you, Sparky. You ruined my kid. He's a nobody because of you. You almost ruined this entire town, too, you, you arsonist. You're a criminal!"

"I've seen your son around town delivering the mail."

"Don't you dare speak with me about my family," said Emil, adding, "Leave! You go right now."

"I've seen your son playing guitar at a bar on Route 14, too, and you know what? Whether he's delivering the mail or picking a tune, he looks like a happy man to me. Not everyone from the 'burbs grows up to be a lawyer or a doctor…or a great basketball player."

John smiled, opened the lid of the garbage can and dropped the entire bag of fresh eggs into the bottom with a wet thud. He still hefted the single egg, and Emil's face froze.

"Oh…you better not!" he screamed.

John dropped the single egg in with the others and walked away. As he left, he said, "And here all these years I thought that I was the pitiful one."

Emil didn't like that at all but John was right.

Emil, and all the others like him, who had given John shit over the years were cowards, never really confronting him face-to-face. They would spout rude comments from across a room, a street or a crowded grocery store, but none of them had really ever spoken directly to John.

The late night, stealthy, egg-throwing escapades cinched it, too. They were weasels. At least John had the idea of going public once his misguided, and yes, now admittedly delusional, "Save the Fourth of July Festival" plan was complete.

Emil, shaking with anger, dragged his garbage can back into his garage.

CHAPTER
- 49 -

Amy was dressed down in an inexpensive, gray-colored pullover and jeans. She sat uncomfortably, and make-up free, in the posh surroundings of the Bistro on Route 14 in Balmoral awaiting John's arrival.

The place was gorgeous, complete with original artwork on the walls, white linens on the tables and a well-dressed and extremely attentive wait staff.

John was late.

She was pissed and didn't want to be there. She was dressed inappropriately for the establishment, but she didn't care one little bit. She was here because, admittedly, she really did need this Kid Crew operation to work out.

She could start her job search all over again, but she didn't want to kid herself. The employment market was brutal. There were no jobs for the getting. She didn't like this at all, but she weighed her options and decided to roll the dice on this dinner date. She didn't have to completely follow through if they did, indeed, wind up back at John's place after dinner.

"He never seemed like that type of guy," she thought as the

waiter poured her another glass of sparkling water.

Wine was offered, but she wanted to keep her head as clear as possible. Who knew where this meeting will all lead. She may have to physically fend for herself after dinner. She didn't want to soften her angry edge with alcohol.

***

"You do exactly what I tell you to do, okay? Exactly how we talked about it. We don't want anyone to get hurt," said John as he and Danny drove in the old station wagon toward the area of Balmoral Road and Route 14.

The sun was setting fast. As they slowly drove past what John had told Danny was a new lumber wholesaler, Danny took a look at the building. All of the front windows were covered in brown paper so no one could get a look inside.

"Is it even open?"

John said, "Yeah, I cased it earlier. That's what I was doing when you saw me with your mom. They've been doing well, so there's got to be some cash there."

"These fuckers are going to shit their pants when we throw down," he laughed.

"Danny, we're doing this my way. We don't scream and yell. We don't showboat. We go in, ask for the money, take the money, and we leave."

"Yeah, sure, whatever."

***

"Hi, Amy," he said.

She was a little startled as she turned and finally noticed Henry standing a few feet away. He was holding a beautiful bouquet of flowers and a large manila envelope. He was dressed in an expensive sport coat, open shirt and trouser ensemble. Amy looked around the room, now very uncomfortable with her evening's clothing choice.

"You look beautiful. May I sit?"

"Sure. I'm waiting for someone, though." She didn't like

the tone she used, so she continued with a softer, "What are you doing here?"

Henry didn't seem thrown by her "waiting for someone" comment one bit. He handed over the flowers, took a seat and motioned to the waiter. As he approached the table, Henry said, "We'll have the Bordeaux now. Thank you."

"I'm not drinking, Henry."

"I think I may be the one you're waiting for, Amy."

***

The traffic on Route 14 was fairly light at this time on a weeknight and John was glad for that.

He and Danny had parked the car two buildings away in the back of the closed car wash. As they prepared to step through the front doors of the Kid Crew/fake lumber wholesaler, John motioned for Danny to pull his baby face mask down over his face. They were both armed with 9mm pistols and dressed in dark blue windbreakers.

"Let's go," said John as he opened the door for Danny. The kid charged into the retail space and accidentally fired a shot directly at Larry's head. Luckily, he had crappy aim.

Larry was able to quickly duck down behind the front counter.

"What the fuck?!" screamed Larry. He knew that the gun was loaded with blanks, but that paper and plastic wadding that rocketed out of the barrel could still do a lot of damage if it hit you in the head.

John grabbed the gun away from Danny and gently said, "Kid, relax, okay. Do it the way we talked about."

John stepped around the counter where he could get a look at Larry to make sure he was okay. Larry gave John a "what the hell" look before he stood up again.

"Okay, don't shoot. I got a family," said Larry, giving John a "was that okay?" expression. John shrugged a little and nodded. Larry punched a button on the cash register and the drawer popped open.

John handed Danny the gun back and said, "Do this."

Danny was a little more careful handling the gun this time.

"Put it all in the bag," said Danny.

But he didn't produce a bag. John cleared his throat and Danny finally understood. He reached into his back pocket and yanked out a plastic grocery bag. Larry took the bag from Danny and began putting the stacks of cash inside.

***

When Henry had arrived at the Bistro he immediately asked the maître d' for the envelopes John said were waiting there for him.

Earlier in the day on the phone, John had advised Henry, "Don't mess this up. This is your shot. Down deep inside she wants this to happen. I'm sure of it. She may not realize it yet, but she will. Treat her with respect or I will hunt you down and hurt you. Are we clear?"

"I love her, John. I won't hurt her."

"I'll be checking up on you from time to time," John said.

Inside the envelope marked with Henry's name was a cashier's check for $100,000 and a handwritten note – "Save your company."

At the table, Henry finally handed Amy the other envelope. As she took control of the envelope, she noticed that her name was handwritten on the front.

"Open it," Henry said.

"What's going on?"

"Go ahead and open it," he said, as he sipped his wine and smiled.

As Amy carefully opened the envelope, the waiter stepped up to the table and delivered two, toaster-sized, gift wrapped boxes. Amy and Henry looked at one another and then to the waiter.

Henry said, "What's this?"

"From an admirer," the waiter said as he stepped away.

So as Amy opened her envelope, Henry tore into the wrapping

around the box in front of him. He opened the box and extracted a small metal sculpture exactly like the ones John had created in his garage from pieces of metal junk.

The sculpture depicted a man sitting in a chair with his hand out to the side. Both Henry and Amy were confused.

Amy said, "What a strange little pile of metal. Go ahead and open the other one."

She then reached into the envelope and extracted a stack of legal papers that were crafted at a law office on East Haddock Place in downtown Chicago. The title of the legal brief was: Sole Ownership Agreement for the Amy Bowling Kid Crew franchise venture.

Henry finally got the other box opened and pulled out a similar piece to the first one. Only this sculpture was a woman sitting in a chair – her hand extended as well. Henry placed the two sculptures side-by-side, and their hands fit perfectly together.

Amy was totally baffled by what was transpiring.

As she allowed the envelope to fall, open side down, on the table, a handwritten note and a single key slid out.

The note read: "You are the sole owner of the Balmoral area Kid Crew. It's all yours free and clear. The rent, utilities, and insurance have been paid in full for the next three years. You may not think that you've earned this, but you have. You've saved my life, Amy, and this is how I'd like to repay you. Be good to Henry. He loves you. Thank you for helping me to get clean and sober."

The note was signed "J."

***

As Larry placed the last of the money, $1,500, into the bag, John tugged on Danny's collar. It was time to leave. But Danny didn't want to go. He stood there and just stared at Larry.

"Come on. Let's get out of here," said John.

John gave Larry a little nod and the dreadlock-wearing man reached back under the counter, coming back up with a sawed-off shotgun.

John forcefully shoved Danny toward the back door of the building as Larry fired off a blank round over their heads.

"Go! Go!" screamed John.

Danny, now scared shitless, finally got the message and bolted toward the back door that John was guiding him towards. John was right behind him.

As they exited the building, a bright light lit up the area.

"On the ground! Get on the ground, now!" ordered Jimmy, standing next to his police cruiser and aiming both his Glock .40 caliber and his car's side spotlight at the robbers.

"Run, kid! Go! Get out of here!" implored John.

And that's exactly what Danny did. Still holding the bag of money, but so frightened that he lost his step and fumbled the gun from his hand, he quickly righted himself and kept on going.

The gun skittered across the parking lot. Danny disappeared into the growing darkness.

Jimmy turned the spotlight off, holstered his gun and said, "Get the guns back by tomorrow. If they find them missing from the property room, I'm toast."

Jimmy didn't say another word as he got into his car and slowly drove away in the opposite direction of the escaping Danny.

"Thanks, brother," said John to no one as he pulled the mask off his head.

He made his way over to where Danny had dropped the gun. John located the weapon and picked it up. As he tucked the gun into his waistband, he stepped back inside the Kid Crew/fake lumber wholesaler. There he found Larry putting his jacket on.

"That went okay," Larry said sarcastically, as John leaned on the counter and took his baby face mask off. "Glad we used blanks. Shit!"

"I owe you," said John.

"Keep the $500, John. You're my friend. I'm glad I was able to help you."

"I owe you more than that."

"Please, John. Dude...there's no need."

John finally relaxed and thought about what he had actually accomplished, and how it had all mostly worked out for the best.

Each and every place that he had stolen money from during his robbery spree was anonymously paid back. With the exception of the breakfast joint in Fox River Grove, which he didn't really steal from, John had paid back his debt the best he could.

The "tidy sum" John had accumulated playing his father's life insurance money in the stock market during the 1990's had, until very recently, grown to a staggering $5,650,000. Of late, that money had dwindled to levels he'd never known in the past, but John was truly happy for probably the first time since he was 10-years-old.

And who was he kidding? He could never be with a woman like Amy. John was too eccentric for her. She was a strong woman who desired to be in charge of her own life and to have a normal existence. She was better matched with Henry, and John was glad for that.

The soon to be reopened Balmoral High School gym would be foundationally sound due to the new cement and structural repairs. The costs for all the repairs would be taken care of by John. Keith Michaels had ordered the signs for the newly-named gym. When the basketball team started their next season, they'd be playing in the "Bernie & Mary Caul Memorial Gymnasium."

The endowment that John had set up with his father's lawyer friend, George, to help perpetually fund the famous Balmoral Fourth of July Festival, was the icing on the cake, though.

That was John's proudest accomplishment.

He hoped that it could maybe smooth out the awkward relationships of other area families, like it had for his own when he was young – even if it only lasted for one week out of the year.

It was a totally anonymous gift. No one would know he had done this, except for the very silent Keith Michaels. Keith swore up and down to the other council members and townspeople that he had no idea who the donor was. He had never seen John's face, so he wasn't really lying.

"It was a cashier's check made out to 'cash,' for crying out loud," he'd say.

It was to be his and the Baby Face Robber's secret to keep.

John and Larry strode outside of the Kid Crew building, and John turned and located the proper key for the door.

As he slid the key into the locking mechanism -- in the northern Indiana town of Merrillville, a state trooper rolled up on Enright's car which sat idle in the far end of a fast-food restaurant's parking lot.

Thirty seconds after the state trooper peered inside the car and saw the carnage of an apparent suicide by shotgun, he radioed into the coroner and his supervisor.

Most of the damage to the victim's face was obscured because he was wearing a creepy, baby face mask. But the top of his head was obliterated. There was shotgun damage to the roof of the car as well, proving that the person had ended his life in this location.

There was a bank bag with a few $20 bills inside from the documented robbery of a breakfast restaurant in the northwest suburbs of Chicago. Also in the car was a typewritten note in size 24 font that read, "Forgive me."

But the oddest thing that would be discovered in the car was the temperature of the body itself. It was nearly frozen to the core, and it smelled of Marinara sauce and Italian sausage for some odd reason.

There were no prints on the vehicle at all, except for the victim's. Jason and Lou had made sure of that when they first checked his driver's license for his address, and then fired the extra shot through the roof of the car. Their final moments with Enright took place when they drove his carcass to the dump site.

John had filed all identifying markings off the 12 gauge shotgun before the Greek brothers transported both Enright's body and his vehicle to Indiana.

Just to be safe, Jason and Lou then circled back to Enright's crappy apartment in the Jefferson Park neighborhood of Chicago to make sure the PI didn't have any hard evidence pointing towards John, Jason, Tyler or Rita.

As they figured, there was nothing there that was incriminating - Enright kept everything in his head and not on paper or elsewhere. They took his laptop just in case and tossed it into the Des Plaines River as they made their way back home in the rental car.

Although there were some strange circumstances to Enright's untimely demise, namely the body temperature and the lack of blood evidence on the inside roof of the car, it didn't take but a moment for the coroner to designate the death a suicide.

Case closed.

CHAPTER
- 50 -

As John sat drinking a glass of milk and eating a piece of warmed-over, frozen pizza in his newly-painted kitchen, his new drug-dealing buddy, Brick, was setting up his first franchise operation in Des Plaines.

Brick had taken John's advice and gone to McCormick Place and taken in the franchise show. There he found every conceivable idea for a business franchise represented at the show.

The company that caught Brick's eye, and also happened to have a low start-up cost, was a hydroponic farming franchise called Hydro-Let Salad, Inc. The business was started in southern California five years prior and was taking off in areas like Chicago, where fresh salads were tougher to find in the winter months.

The company specialized in providing upscale restaurants the greens that their discerning customers required time and time again and year-round, as well.

Brick was in the high-end, hydroponic salad business as soon as he handed over his check to the Hydro-Let Salad, Inc. representative.

MATT HADER

From his unassuming warehouse on Touhy Avenue in Des Plaines, he would grow the arugula, bibb lettuce and romaine hearts the wealthy customers of upscale restaurants all over the Chicago area would yearn for.

Sure, he'd be growing some prime California blue mystic marijuana right next to the bibb lettuce, but Brick was slowly becoming a legitimate businessman.

***

In John's kitchen, the roosters and apple motif was gone, but he'd hired Larry to replace them with his unique versions soon enough. Hell, maybe he'd even spring for new cabinets, countertops and flooring, as well.

He had just gotten home from his fake robbery and was just settling down so he could get some needed sleep when the front doorbell chimed.

Crossing the living room to answer the door, John could see out the front window and noticed a car drive slowly past. It was a dark-colored Crown Victoria. The car stopped and idled for just a moment and then drove away.

John opened the door to find a terrified Danny standing there and sucking in gulps of air. John grabbed him by the windbreaker and tugged him into the house. He led the teenager to the kitchen and sat him down.

"I...ran...this...whole...time," said Danny, as he yanked the bag of money and a crushed baby face mask out of his waistband.

Danny wasn't embellishing, either.

He had literally been running all around the town of Balmoral for the past hour. First, he ran westbound along the back of the commercial buildings on Route 14. After a couple of blocks, he crossed over the highway and sprinted through the park, hoping the darkness would camouflage him from any police who were searching for him.

He lost his step a couple of times as he paralleled the freight train tracks and had to angle in a different direction, when yet another train came rocketing through town.

After being separated at the scene of the robbery, his goal was always to just back home. But when he did finally arrive at his back door, he saw through the large windows of the great room, that Sharon and Donald, his mom and dad, were on the sofa making out like a couple of horny teenagers.

"Shit. Gross, man…" said Danny as he ran away, yet again.

Danny didn't realize it, but Sharon and Donald had had a session just that afternoon with a marriage counselor in Cary.

The argument they had at the counselor's office was a robust one, too. There was a lot of screaming, shouting, and finger pointing as to which partner had caused the major rift in their marriage.

After they got home, though, Sharon and Donald were so full of adrenaline, anger, and angst that it totally turned them on. After ripping each other's clothes off, they wound up making love in nearly every room of the house. Danny saw them just as they were about to christen the great room.

Danny's next move was getting to John's house. He really couldn't believe that he had made it, either, especially after being chased down by the hulking teen, Staley, and a couple of his drunken buddies after leaving his own home. Staley saw Danny sprinting across Grove Street and gave chase.

"You can run, fuck-stick, but you can't hide," yelled Staley as Danny made a perilous decision, sprinting between two moving vehicles on busy Balmoral Road. Staley and his two buddies were drunk, but they were smart enough not to risk their lives to catch up with the smartass Danny.

Now sitting at John's kitchen table, Danny was so happy to be safe that he felt like crying, but that wouldn't be a cool move to make around the older dude, John.

John got him a cold glass of water from a jug in the fridge and sat down. Danny gulped down the water between deep breaths.

"Take it easy, Danny. Breathe," said John.

Danny pushed the bag of money across the kitchen table but

John pushed it right back and said, "It's yours."

"Shit, that was close. I thought you got caught! How did you get away?"

"When we both ran in different directions, he went after you, but you were too fast for him, I'd guess," said John.

"And that fucker with the shotgun, what the hell? What the fuck, man! Shit, I lost the gun! Holy shit, I lost the gun!"

"There were no markings on it, so don't worry about it. It's okay."

John allowed the kid to relax and settle down. He didn't like him being in his house, but what could he do about it now.

What John didn't know was that Shane Thompson, the Paladin police detective, was sitting just down the block in the very same Crown Victoria that had just rolled past.

Thompson wasn't on official business just yet, but he had a solid, gut feeling that John Caul was the Baby Face Robber. He also wondered if he'd be able to brace the kid who had just stepped into his suspect's home so he could get more information.

Thompson figured that he would snatch the kid up when he finally left the house. Since no one at his department knew that he was in Balmoral working this case on his own, he may be able to stretch the usual rules of interrogation when he confronted the kid.

The teen would talk, he was sure of it. Then he'd be closer to grabbing the Baby Face Robber's proceeds all for himself.

His overtime pay had dwindled to nearly zero in the past few years. The police department had unofficially traded chasing criminals for writing as many citations as possible. Detectives didn't write citations. The new policy would help to pump up the suburb's coffers during the economic down times, but the new direction of the department played havoc on Shane Thompson's personal bank account.

Nabbing the Baby Face Robber was his lost overtime pay equalizer. Shane Thompson would finally be able to purchase that sweet new BMW he had his eye on.

Danny drank heartily from the glass of water, his breathing slowing down to a more normal pace.

"I'm scared, John."

"It's going to be just fine."

"No, you don't understand, I'm really afraid."

"I get it, Danny. That was a traumatic thing being shot at and then having a cop almost catch you like that. I get it. Now you see why I didn't want you to do this? It's a crazy and stupid thing to do. You could get killed. Or worse, you could hurt someone that you don't even know. An innocent person. You really don't want to live with the consequences of that, do you?"

John thought he had calmed the kid down enough and that his plan to scare Danny straight was accomplished. He'd finally be able to map out his next life move.

He'd probably start by aggressively playing the stock market so he could pad his bank accounts once again.

Then what?

He didn't quite know just yet. He did know that he'd be staying right there in Balmoral. It was his home. If someone was going to be a smartass and call him Sparky from time to time, so be it. He had put up with it for the past 20 years, what difference would it make now? He had actually grown so accustomed to the nickname that it was starting to grow on him.

He'd find another woman to date. There were hundreds of them out in the world. He'd start his search in the themed-restaurant bars around the Woodfield Mall area. There were many fish in that sea called Woodfield Mall.

"I'm afraid, man."

"Okay, take it easy," said John.

"I'm afraid that I want to do it again!"

"What?"

"John, I've been thinking. If we don't do another robbery, I am definitely telling the cops what you've been up to. You can fucking bank on it, man," said Danny, smiling from ear to ear.

"Wait, what?"

Danny was elated just thinking about his future prospects, and said, "Who should we hit next? How about an armored car? No. First a bank. That would be so cool. Then we'll do an armored car!"

John couldn't correctly form all of his thoughts into words. All he could say was, "But. But. But…" And all he could really think was, "I wonder if I have any Vicodin left in the house."

ABOUT THE AUTHOR

Matt Hader enjoys cooking, long evening strolls on the beach with his lovely wife, drives through the countryside, building papier-mache' busts of famous inventors, studying archeology, browsing farmer's markets, tinkering in his human reanimation laboratory, designing botanical gardens, spelunking, using sentences with many, many commas in them, and making stuff up. He splits his time between the Chicago and San Francisco Bay areas.

CPSIA information can be obtained at www.ICGtesting.com
Printed in the USA
LVOW060232261011

252116LV00002B/2/P